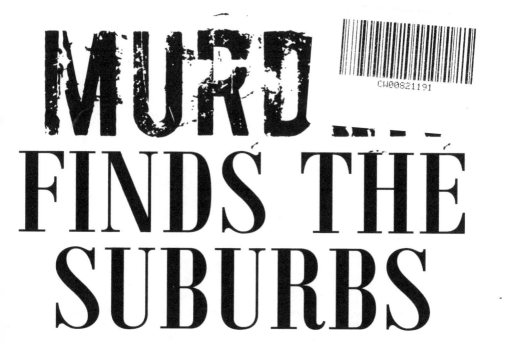

MURD...
FINDS THE
SUBURBS

LOUIS A. DORIO

outskirts
press

Outskirts Press, Inc.
http://www.outskirtspress.com

ISBN: 978-1-9772-1553-6

Cover Image by Louis A. Dorio

Outskirts Press and the "OP" logo are trademarks belonging to Outskirts Press, Inc.

PRINTED IN THE UNITED STATES OF AMERICA

Acknowledgements

I would like to thank my beautiful wife for her encouragement and support in my pursuit to create this novel. Her insight, understanding and helpful editing helped me through what turned out to be an enjoyable and fulfilling project.

A special thanks to my good friend, Louis Conte. Louis also worked in the field of Criminal Justice as an Assistant Commissioner of Probation for Westchester County and helped me put my thoughts and ideas to paper.

Thank you to my professional editor Patti Manzi who helped a first time writer become an author.

Dedication

I am dedicating this book to the memory of my Mother and Father. They instilled in me a strong sense of integrity and love of family.

'Two anonymous lifeless bodies lie on the hard-frozen ground alongside a small winding road in an affluent suburban town, north of the confines of New York City. The discovery of the bodies will result in an awakening of the sleepy bedroom community's police department and one of the agency's young, upstart police officers.'

CHAPTER 1

O ne brisk Monday morning in early March 1984, I began a coveted rotation in the Detective Division of the Lakeside Police Department. Thanks to television and movies, detectives are portrayed as the elite members of the department and are held in the highest regard. While TV and movie portrayals make for good entertainment, they are not accurate portrayals of detectives in the real world. Real detectives are hardworking police officers and far less glamorous than their celebrity counterparts would suggest.

Chief Stephen Silver, a distinguished-looking man who invariably projected a highly polished, professional appearance called me into his office and motioned for me to have a seat. "DeMarco, since you're in line for an upcoming promotion to sergeant, I'm putting you in the detective division. You'll broaden your experience."

"Am I going into this assignment as a detective, Chief?" I wanted that gold badge, proof of earning the rank of detective.

"No Rocco, because it's only a temporary assignment, you'll be in the Detective Bureau as a patrolman."

I felt some disappointment of not getting a gold shield, however, the prospective promotion was good news; I was anxious to leave the County Police and work my way up the police ladder. "Do you have a timetable for the promotion, Chief?"

"Not yet, I'm waiting for Sergeant Winston to finally decide about his retirement."

Even though Winston constantly complained about the

job that he was lucky to have and was not good at, it appeared as though someone was going to have to "pry his cold dead hands off the door handle" or push him out.

"What's my promotion got to do with the bureau?"

"Lieutenant Capanno's regular hours are 9 – 5, Monday to Friday." The Chief gulped some coffee. "Coverage for the hours when Randy isn't around falls to the shift officer. In other words, you." He sat back in his chair. "I would like to see if some young blood could spark those dinosaurs in the bureau to get something done for a change."

I'd been with the Lakeside Police Department for approximately seven years. I started my police career with the Westchester County Police, an agency whose primary function was highway patrol and vehicle and traffic enforcement. After six months, I transferred to Lakeside, seeking more diverse police duties and the challenges of protecting people in a community.

Despite not going in as a gold shield, I was ready for this opportunity in the detective division.

Sergeant Frank McGill, a likeable man in his 50's who looked like a beardless Santa Claus, was the PBA President of the County Police. He approached me in the locker room as I was getting ready to leave for my new assignment. "Rocco, I thought you liked it here."

"I do. But I really don't want to be a highway patrol officer; it's time for me to try something different. There's a pay raise, too, Frank."

McGill nodded.

"I'm married with a kid and three thousand dollars more is a lot of money. But it's really more about the diversity of duties than the money."

"I get it, but you might have a better chance for advancement here," McGill added.

"Lakeside isn't that small, Sarge. I think I could do okay there."

By national standards, the Lakeside Police Department is not considered a small department, with seventy-three police men and women officers; eighty percent of the police departments in the United States have fewer than twenty-five officers. However, when compared to the New York City PD, its big brother a short distance to the south, it is considered tiny. The NYPD has thirty-eight thousand officers. Some criminal justice critics believe departments like Lakeside's are not capable of handling major cases.

In fact, some of those critics are members of the Lakeside Police Department.

Lakeside is a suburban town in Westchester County, New York, just a short train ride from New York City on the New Haven line of the Metro North Railroad. There are numerous highways that connect the town to other parts of Westchester County and Connecticut.

Commuters make up the fabric of Lakeside. Residents who work in New York City return to Lakeside's peaceful surroundings weekday evenings. This "bedroom community" of twenty-two square miles has a population of approximately twenty-five thousand. However, that number swells to nearly two-hundred thousand during the day, thanks to those working for large, prestigious corporations headquartered in town. The community has three colleges and a significant part of the Westchester County Airport.

Lakeside is a wealthy community with six country clubs and many sprawling estates. The town also has its pockets of working-class families, many of whom are of Italian descent, like me.

While the town has had *some* serious crimes over the years, they have been on an increase recently. Lakeside residents often say "that isn't supposed to happen here" or "those things don't happen in this town."

Except sometimes, they do.

One of the benefits of working in Lakeside is that the investigating officers have the opportunity to practice the many different facets of crime-solving. We learn to be generalists rather than the specialists more common in larger agencies. For example, in a homicide investigation, a Lakeside detective is responsible for most aspects of the investigation – from photography, evidence collection, and crime scene processing, right up to interrogating, arresting and processing.

In recent years, officers have had their chance to hone their investigative skills in high profile cases such as the murder of Dr. Hightower, a prominent diet doctor. Another case which attracted national attention was the arson of a local hotel in which twenty-six people died and scores of others were injured. Although that arson investigation was one that would have presented a challenge to the largest of departments, it was handled professionally by our Lakeside Police Department.

The following is the story about my first homicide case in the Lakeside Police Department Detective Division.

May 1977

Right after transferring to Lakeside, it didn't take long to learn how busy this seemingly quiet community police department is.

Since I was the new guy, Sergeant Winston assigned me to patrol downtown: a park and walk job. Winston knew I didn't know the town well yet, and of the twenty-six square miles of Lakeside, the downtown area was the easiest sector to learn.

"DeMarco, remember to keep your car close in the event you're needed for a back-up," Sergeant Winston advised.

"Remember, the reason we have you walking is to give you a chance to get to know the business people and give them a chance to know you. You'll also figure out who's got the best coffee and doughnuts." Winston winked.

"Got it, Sarge."

"One more thing. Here's the key for the traffic light control box across from the railroad lot. Remember how it works?"

"Yes, flip the switch to put the light on *manual*. Use the button on the end of the cord to cycle the light."

One of my duties was to manage traffic at the railroad station parking lot. The lot became congested when the evening trains arrived from New York City. The light was normally on a blinking cycle: the train lot side blinking red and the street side blinking "caution," yellow. To clear the cars picking up commuters from the lot, the officer changes the signals so exiting cars have the green go-ahead and the street side, a red signal. I was met at the traffic box by Officer Rosen and Sergeant Harrison, the road sergeant.

"Hey, Rosen, tell the kid what happens on the railroad traffic detail." Officer Rosen laughed.

"DeMarco, you have to remember that most of the people using that road are used to the light blinking yellow," Harrison explained.

"You'll hear the tires screeching and the sound of crunching metal." Rosen added, "It sure can get entertaining."

"So," I nodded and smiled, "I'm doing this detail for entertainment?"

Sergeant Harrison made me wipe the smile off my face, "No you're doing it to get the people picking up the commuters out of the damn parking lot so that we're not dealing with them whining to the Town Supervisor about the traffic." Then he added with his own smile, "The entertainment is an added perk."

No sooner than I began to enjoy the rhythm of the railroad traffic, when I received a transmission on my portable radio – a *hot line* announcement from a neighboring department.

Hot line announcements go out to multiple agencies simultaneously to solicit back-up help.

The alert came from the nearby Rockwood Police Department, "All units on the hot line, this agency had an armed robbery five minutes ago at the Sunnyside Service Station located on Homestead Avenue. Subjects described as male blacks, approximately 20 – 25 years of age, wearing black hooded sweatshirts, last seen heading on foot toward the downtown section of Lakeside. Subjects are armed with what appeared to be chrome handguns."

In an effort to get his rookie cop out of the way, the patrol sergeant ordered me to proceed to Oakdale Lane, a dead-end street. One of the unstated rules in police work is that you don't get new hires killed on their first patrol. It reflects poorly on the department.

"Rocco, go down to the dead-end of Oakdale. It's next to a wooded area. I'm betting these mutts will try to stay off the main roads if they can."

As I neared Oakdale, I saw one of the detective division's unmarked cars with two of the department's detective lieutenants sitting inside.

I also saw two individuals matching the descriptions of those on the hot-line running through the wooded area adjacent to Oakdale, heading toward Butcher Avenue, a block away. I cut a sharp right turn onto Willow Street, traveling in the wrong direction on a one-way street.

As I said, I didn't know the area very well yet.

At Butcher Avenue, I saw the two subjects running into a driveway. I quickly pulled my patrol car up to the driveway and shut the engine as one of the men tried to hide behind a low bush. The other subject continued to run. I jumped from the car, drew my revolver and positioned myself behind a large tree for protection from a bullet.

"You, behind the bush!" I shouted, "Come out with your hands up. I'm not going to ask you twice."

The subject emerged, hands up. I could see the handgun in his waist band. Maintaining my position of cover behind the tree, I ordered him to place his hands on the tree next to where he was standing and spread his legs. When he complied, I disarmed him, cuffed him and pushed him into the back of my patrol car.

Lieutenant Simpson arrived, huffing and puffing after the run from his unmarked car. "Where'd he go, Kid?"

"Lieutenant, he's sitting in the back of my car."

Still panting, he asked, "Why didn't you call it in?"

"Cause I have no idea what street I'm on."

The next day I was back at the railroad parking lot detail.

CHAPTER 2

I began my police career in 1976, at twenty-eight, after serving on an aircraft carrier during the Vietnam War. Twenty-eight is a bit older than many of my fellow officers were when they started their own police careers.

Shortly after my discharge from the Navy, I got married and my wife, Audrey, and I started our family. I worked for a while in the telecommunications industry and in graphic arts.

My interest in police work was sparked by a recruitment presentation I attended after my tour of duty in Vietnam. It was given by a member of the California Highway Patrol (CHiPS) at a Naval base in San Francisco.

I approached the officer after his presentation. "That sounds like something I would be very interested in."

There was just one problem.

The officer looked down at me and grinned. "How tall are you, boy?"

"Five-foot eight, sir."

"Sorry Kid, but our height requirement is six foot."

I was tall enough to go to Vietnam but too short to be a cop.

I forgot about becoming a member of CHiPS and returned home to New York.

I decided to check with the City of White Plains, where I grew up, to see about their height requirement for police officers.

Five-foot ten.

Becoming a police officer, I figured, just wasn't in the

cards. After working as a shoe salesman, I took a job with a telecommunications company.

During a lunch break one day, a co-worker came into the break room and exclaimed, "I got it!"

"You got what, Pete?"

"I got the police job in Mayville Village." Mayville was a small village in Westchester County.

"Whoa. Come here a minute. Stand back to back with me." I called another buddy over. "Hey, Joe, is Pete any taller than I am?"

"You guys look the same to me."

"White Plains told me the height was five-foot ten," I said. "You're not five-foot ten."

"It's not five-ten for the towns and villages – it's five-eight," he beamed.

I took the civil service tests, scored near the top on each one and was quickly hired by the Westchester County Police.

Monday, March 5th 1984

When I started my rotation in the detective division, I was 35 years old. My lieutenant, who strived for perfection in all that he did, was ten years my senior and aside from me, the young-ster in the division. The rest of the detectives were a bunch of dinosaurs who were at least twelve years past retirement age.

My cases accumulated from day one, despite the fact that I was the new "kid." I was given two active burglary cases.

During my third day in the bureau, the lieutenant had me double up with Detective Henry Roberts, who had been on the job for thirty-five years. Roberts was a large man with a boom-ing voice and when he decided to make the center of the room his stage, one could not help but notice him.

"So, you're here because Silver is thinking of making you sergeant?" Roberts said. "How long are you on the job?"

"Seven years."

"Seven years?" he grumbled. "You shouldn't have even been allowed to take the sergeant's test till you had ten years in."

Most of the more senior officers, detectives and even patrol officers are of the opinion promotions and special assignments should be based on time in service rather than on skill or merit.

Roberts pulled no punches when telling me how little respect he had for our lieutenant. When Lieutenant Capanno wasn't around, Roberts frequently made comments imitating him and mocking his reasoned, thoughtful approach to conducting investigations.

Roberts would stand in the middle of the room with his thumb and forefinger on his chin to mimic Capanno, "Hmmm, what type of crime do we have here? Is it a crime of chance or a crime of opportunity?"

I wasn't sure if the lieutenant ever caught any of Roberts' acts but right after one performance, the lieutenant came into the squad room. Roberts could care less. "Henry, I want you to follow up with Mrs. Carlson on her reported burglary. It's important for you to see her right away to get her stolen property depositions."

"Got it Lieu, I'll see her right away. Let's go, Kid."

"Doesn't Mrs. Carlson live on Ridge Road?" Roberts was driving in the opposite direction.

"Yup."

"So where are we going?"

"To get a cup of coffee."

Regardless of how many cases Detective Roberts had or how pressing the case was, he started his day with a stop at a local deli for a cookie and a cup of coffee. He drove to the same street, parked his car in his favorite location under the shade of a willow tree, and leisurely enjoyed his coffee and cookie.

This day was no exception to Roberts's routine.

"Want a coffee, Kid?"

"No thanks, Henry."

"How about a cookie?"

"I'm good. Thanks."

Sensing I was not enjoying the leisure time as much as he was, Roberts asked, "What's the matter, Kid, you got ants in your pants?"

"No, but I have some work to do on two burglary cases."

"Relax, Kid, the cases will be there when we get back. Besides, if you do what we do and write them up as larcenies it will be less work for you."

"But they're burglaries."

"And what do you think your chances of solving them are?"

"I'm not sure."

"Remember, Kid, better an unsolved bullshit larceny than a burglary."

This was not my way of doing my job.

CHAPTER 3

Thursday, March 8th

Fortunately for me, Thursday, March 8th was Detective Roberts' day off. I was on my own. The lieutenant was showing me a new film that had just come in for the 35mm camera. The 35mm required more work in processing but resulted in better images. The dinosaurs, of course, preferred the old Graflex camera.

"Rocco, I know the others have been trying to pawn off as much of the film processing as possible on you."

"Yeah, but I don't mind. It's not that difficult."

"It's not so much the difficulty as it is sheer laziness. When they found out about your graphic arts experience, they were overjoyed."

The film we were evaluating was a 35mm color instant slide film developed by Polaroid. Each roll came with a developer pack which, when combined with the exposed roll of film and processed through a small processing unit, produced a roll of color slides which could then be cut to size and placed in slide holders.

I looked at the instructions. "Seems simple enough to figure out, the film itself is loaded in the camera the traditional way. The 64 ASA should produce crisp slides if the light is bright enough."

"OK Rocco, you lost me on that one. The 64 what?"

"64 ASA is the speed of the film. Most of the black and

white stuff we shoot with the old Graflex and the 35mm is 200 or 400 ASA, which requires less light, but when the print is made into 8x10 from the negative it isn't as sharp and loses some detail."

"I'm going to take a roll for practice to see how they look and to fine tune camera settings. Let me expose a roll by taking some trial shots and we'll have a look."

As I was trying to master the new film, just a short distance away there were two County highway workers picking up trash bags left on the side of the road.

The men were on Lincoln Road when they saw a couple of large, green plastic trash bags. Not in any rush, they slowly put their gloves on and climbed down from their truck. The driver said, "Come on Frank let's go see what garbage people are throwing on the side of the road this time. Maybe we'll find something good."

"Right. Remember the time we found a bag with almost-new power tools in it? Who knows what stuff the people are throwing away?"

Frank climbed over the guard rail to reach the bags. When he attempted to lift the closest one, Frank shouted, "Shit! What the hell is in here?"

He tried to drag the bag closer to the rail where his partner was standing. "This fucking thing is heavy. I'm going to cut it open to see what's inside."

As he continued to bitch about the bulk, Frank sliced through one of the bags. "Holy shit! Bill! There's a body in here! Go back to the truck and radio for the cops!"

I was just finishing my trial run with the new film when the lieutenant shouted, "Grab a bunch of rolls and the camera! We have a case on Lincoln Road, across the street from Lakeside High School."

At the scene, the lieutenant and I joined the police officers who had already roped off the area with yellow crime scene tape. Captain Johnston, a tall handsome man and one who, like Lieutenant Capanno, took pride in his appearance and his work.

Captain Johnston greeted us and was quick to explain, "Those guys up the street near the County highway truck were picking up bags along the road when they got to these two bags. When the bag was too heavy to lift, one of them cut it open and saw a dead girl inside."

"Did he touch the other bag?" Capanno asked.

"No, they figured it was best not to and called for us instead. Amazingly enough, our first officer on the scene, Rosen, had the sense not to touch the other bag either. He had the County guys move their truck up the road and roped off the scene."

The crime scene was directly across from Lakeside High School. It was a relatively narrow road with one lane in each direction and many curves and bends. Lincoln Road is in close proximity to two major highways, Interstate 95 and the Hutchinson River Parkway. The police activity quickly attracted attention. Controlling the onlookers and the kids leaving the high school for the day, the tasks of directing traffic and keeping the scene secure were more than difficult.

"Captain, has the M.E's office been notified?" I asked.

"Yes, they are on their way. We'll let them open the second bag."

As I was waiting for the Medical Examiner to arrive, I loaded my camera and began documenting the scene and the surrounding area.

It didn't take long before the local newspaper reporters and photographers arrived. While the purpose of my photography was to document and later use to solve the case, the media's photos were intended to sell newspapers with sensational shots to emphasize the grizzly nature of the crime.

After all, "these things don't happen here."

I turned to Captain Johnston, "I want to photograph the

side of the road adjacent to the area where the bags are for tire tracks. Aside from the County truck tire tracks, were the police vehicles close to this location?"

"Rosen parked his car across the street where it is now and the other units were parked away from this spot as well. You think you're going to get anything useful?"

"Better safe than sorry, especially until we find out how long the bags have been here."

The discovery of the bodies, which turned out to be one in each of the two plastic bags, occurred on a brisk March day. It hadn't snowed for several weeks, and the lack of any snow cover contributed to the difficulty of determining how long the bodies may have been at this location.

In short order, the medical examiner arrived. Dr. Anderson, an accomplished Forensic Pathologist, took as much pleasure bragging about his golf game as he did his medical expertise. He confirmed with Lieutenant Capanno that the second bag had not been opened.

"We haven't touched anything, Doc. I have an officer ready with a video camera to document the opening of the second bag; Officer DeMarco is taking still photos."

"Very good, Lieutenant. I'm glad we've learned from past mistakes, to not let history repeat itself."

This was a dig from the doctor referencing the murder case that took place a few years back. Mistakes were made by the police, the majority by seasoned detectives and superior officers. Doctor Anderson made a comment after the trial was over that, "The police were lucky to get a conviction in spite of their police work and not a result of it." In fact, there were those saying that the FBI in Quantico used that case as an example of how *not* to investigate a homicide.

Dr. Anderson opened the second bag. There was the second body.

Then one of his assistants said, "Oh look it's another babe." The voice recorder was on, as well as video. This off the cuff remark was going to make it highly unlikely the video could be used.

Lieutenant Capanno said "I guess we *all* are capable of making mistakes."

Dr. Anderson did a preliminary inspection to determine how long the bodies may have been there. He said that one victim appeared to be black, possibly Hispanic, late teens to early 20's and the other victim looked to be Hispanic, mid to late 20's. He noted that there did not appear to be much in the way of decomposition but explained the cold temperatures could have contributed to the preserved condition of the bodies. That prompted me to check with the weather service for temperatures prior to the discoveries.

Once the bodies were loaded into the medical examiner's van, the deep impressions left on the ground by the bags indicated they were not recently dumped.

"It looks as though they may have been here for some time," I said. "The ground is hard now; the weight of those two victims could not have made these impressions recently."

"You're right, Rocco. Looks like the photos you took of tire marks may not be of much evidentiary value," Lieutenant Capanno added.

"It was a stroke of good luck that we got this new film this week, Lieu."

"Why's that?"

"I can process it right here on the spot and make sure I got everything before the tape is removed and the scene is released."

Lieutenant Capanno turned to me and said, *"This is your case, Kid."*

Four days in the detective division and still a patrolman, I had been handed a double homicide case.

CHAPTER 4

Lola was sitting on the cold steps of Bronx P.S. 117 High School, uncomfortable both from the chill of the concrete steps and from the thought of how her friend-would take the news of her plans to go into the Army. Lola worked part-time as a clerk in a Dollar Store on Southern Boulevard and since her hours generally coincided with Crystal's school day, she often met her friend at the school to make sure she was attending classes. Crystal always looked forward to seeing her older friend, who made the five-year difference in their ages disappear when they were together.

That Thursday, the school day had just ended, Lola saw Crystal leading the group of exiting teenagers.

Crystal ran to her friend and gave her a big hug, as she typically did. Then she paused, "Lola, what's the matter? You look so serious."

Lola looked down to avoid Crystal's eyes. "I really shouldn't look serious, I should look happy, but I have some news I'm not sure you'll like."

"What could you possibly have to tell me that I won't like?"

"I've decided to enlist in the Army. I've been thinking about it since I passed the GED. I met with a recruiter a few months ago, and he told me that without a high school diploma or a GED I couldn't get in. I didn't tell you back then because I wasn't even sure I'd pass the test."

Hoping to get Crystal to understand, she said, "Crystal you know how much I hate living with my mother and the best job I have been able to get without my high school diploma is this dead-end job at the Dollar Store."

Crystal was obviously surprised but tried not to show her friend how sad she felt.

"You can come live with me; you don't have to join the Army."

"First of all, your mother and step-father don't need another mouth to feed and second, the Army will give me training so when I get out, I can get a better job. I want a better life, Crystal; I'm twenty years old and feel as if I'm going nowhere. Don't worry. I'm not going to stay in the Army forever."

"How long before you have to go?" Crystal asked.

"I don't have to leave until the end of the month. Basic training is only ten weeks and they say the time will go by very fast. I'll write to you every day."

Crystal put on a smile and took Lola's hand, "Let's have a GED party and a going away party combined. I have to get home right now, but we can plan the party later or tomorrow."

Both girls lived in the Bronx, relatively close to each other. Lola lived on Simpson Street, the same street as the NYPD 41st Precinct. Back in the day, the 41st was known as "Fort Apache" due to the almost constant violence in the neighborhood. Eventually it became known as the "Little House on The Prairie" because so many of the surrounding buildings were lost to abandonment and destruction. Lola's apartment building was one of the few remaining intact structures on Simpson Street. Crystal lived a few blocks away in a housing project on 161st Street, near the corner of Union Avenue. Both Crystal and Lola were hardened Bronx girls who had relied on each other for safety and companionship.

Crystal arrived home, still thinking about her friend's news, in time to say goodbye to her stepfather, Francisco Ramos, who was just leaving for his job as a meatpacker in

Hunts Point; he held a second job as a custodian in an old building on Southern Blvd. The jobs seemed to be taking a toll on him physically, but Crystal knew he worked hard so that one day he could move the family into a bigger apartment in a better neighborhood. Crystal had two younger step-brothers; as the older sister, Crystal often took on some mothering duties to help her mother. Her responsibilities made her think of herself as being more mature than her 15 years allowed.

That same afternoon, Lola, while in no rush to get home, did so because the weather was getting colder. Lola lived with her mother, who got by on public assistance. She depended on Lola's low-paying job for financial help. Lola barely brought home enough money to make ends meet, let alone support her mother's drinking and gambling habits.

"Where have you been Lola? I've been waiting for you. I need something from the store."

Lola put her hands on her hips and shook her head in disgust.

"What do you need this time, vodka, cigarettes?"

Her mother lit a cigarette, glared and inhaled some smoke. "I need both."

Lola hung up her coat, I'm going into the Army at the end of this month."

"You can't go in the Army! I didn't sign anything."

"You don't need to sign anything, I'm twenty years old and I don't need your permission."

Her mother coughed as she exhaled, "So, now the Army is taking high school drop-outs?"

"I'm no longer a drop-out. I got my GED."

"How much does the Army pay you?"

"I don't know yet, but you won't get any of it. I gave you my Dollar Store money because I've been living here. Ask your dead-beat husband and son to help you. Oh, that's right – they can't. Those two assholes got locked up for robbing other drug dealers."

"So, you're going to leave me on my own?"

"You're a grown woman, you'll manage."

CHAPTER 5

Friday, February 3rd

Crystal went to school every day because, as much as she hated being there, she did so not to disappoint Lola. She knew Lola wanted her to graduate and have the advantages that a diploma would offer. She was looking at the clock and waiting for the bell to ring. It was Friday and she had a party to plan.

Lola was waiting outside the school at the end of the day, as usual. She knew how excited Crystal was about planning her GED/Army party. In truth, she was excited as well.

The bell rang and Crystal was out the door like a race horse leaving the starting gate.

Lola called to her, "Crystal, over here. How was school?"

"It sucks," Crystal smiled, "I go because I know you would be mad if I didn't. I'm not learning shit."

"Well, just think of the future. You'll be finished with school. I'll be finished with the Army. Maybe we can both get out of this crappy neighborhood."

"Let's not think about any of that now. We have a party to plan. Let's go to Manny's Bodega on Southern Blvd."

"OK! Let's get out of the cold, Crystal. I'm actually looking forward to basic training in Georgia, where the winters are warmer."

Manny's had a couple of small tables in the rear, where Lola and Crystal sat down to splurge on soda and crumb cakes.

"What day do you actually have to leave for the Army?" Crystal asked between a sip of soda and a bite of cake.

"Monday, the 20th."

"That doesn't leave us much time to plan this party! Where should we have it?" She thought for a moment. "Let's try to have it at Danny's father's club. It's right in the neighborhood and our friends know where it is."

Lola didn't want to disappoint her friend because she seemed so excited, but she really didn't like that club. "Crystal, that club really gets crowded sometimes." She took a bite of crumb cake, "You know the kind of men that go in there."

Crystal didn't get it. "It's early now. I don't think many people will be there, so let's go see what Danny says. He likes you, Lola, so he may want to help out with your party. If we see any disgusting old men when we get there, we can go back another time."

When the girls knocked on the door, Danny peered through the small window on the door to see who would be there before opening hours. Seeing Lola and Crystal, he pulled the door open and welcomed the pretty girls inside, as though inviting them into a swanky nightclub.

They were happy to learn that Danny was alone.

"What are you girls doing here?"

"Lola just got her GED and is going into the Army. We want to have a party for her."

"What kind of party were you thinking about?"

"Just a few of our friends, with a little food, some beer and some other stuff for the older kids, if we can get some."

"I don't think it would be a problem, but we have to ask my father when he gets back."

Lola and Crystal knew that Danny was slow-witted. He was twenty-three years old and acted more like an immature kid than a grown man. Had it not been for his father, who took care of him, Danny would not have amounted to much, not that working in this dingy hole was much. Pablo, Danny's father, tried to protect his son from the cruel taunts of the low-end regulars whose business kept the club going.

Lola took Danny aside as Crystal was looking around, planning how to set up for the party. Lola whispered so her friend wouldn't overhear how much she really didn't want to be there, "Danny, we don't want to have your father's regulars here while we're having this party. Most of my older friends can take care of themselves with those slime balls, but Crystal is only 15 years old."

She wondered if Danny understood.

CHAPTER 6

C rystal was waiting for Lola to come over so they could go to the club to make the final arrangements for the party.

The Ramos apartment was small with a kitchen, a bathroom and two bedrooms, which meant Crystal had to share a bedroom with her step-brothers. Crystal's mother, Maria, took pride in making the apartment clean and presentable. The furniture was old, but Mrs. Ramos managed to make the apartment comfortable and not one she was ashamed of.

Crystal came into the kitchen as her mother was cleaning up. Mrs. Ramos looked up at her daughter and said, "Crystal, es muy frío."

"I know it's cold out, Momma."

"Tu chaqueta no es muy cálido."

"Momma, the jacket is fine. I'm not going to be outside that much. My teachers in school say you should use English more often to learn it."

Maria Ramos was younger than her appearance would suggest. Life in the neighborhood was hard and trying to provide a normal life for her family had taken its toll, yet she remained an attractive woman. Mrs. Ramos knew the neighborhood was forcing Crystal to age beyond her years. But this was still her baby and she did whatever she could to protect her.

"Momma, I love this sweater and it is warm enough." She

spun around as though modeling a mink coat and danced to open the door.

When Lola entered, Mrs. Ramos smiled. "Olá, Lola, cómo estás? Lo siento, how are you? Crystal says I should use English more."

"I'm fine, thank you Mrs. Ramos. I guess Crystal is taking some of the things she learns in school home," Lola winked at her friend.

Mrs. Ramos said, "Is good job getting the GED. Good for you, Lola! You are not afraid to go in the Army?"

"No, I'll be fine. I hope I can get a better job when I get out. I'll be writing to Crystal all the time to make sure she is going to school and staying out of trouble," Lola smiled and gave another wink in Crystal's direction.

Mrs. Ramos got Crystal's camera and took pictures of the two girls together. She knew how much her daughter liked taking pictures and asked if she was taking her camera out today.

"No camera today momma we are going to plan a party."

"Hace mucho frío. Por favor, llegues a casa temprano. I am sorry...please come home early because it is very cold...or wear a warm coat."

"Very good mama. You are getting better with English," Crystal said with affection, "but I don't want to wear a coat. We won't be out late. C'mon Lola let's go."

The girls went out onto the cold streets of the Bronx.

CHAPTER 7

E arly that Saturday afternoon, Lola and Crystal arrived at the club as Pablo and Danny were unlocking the door. The girls knew that meant the club was empty and they would not have to fend off lecherous men. The social club had no semblance to anything people might consider upscale.

The entrance was a single door that led down a narrow set of stairs to the windowless club. The stairs were dark, due to lack of lighting as well as the broken street light outside. Had the streetlight been repaired, someone would have broken it again. The locks on the club's doors were proof of the unsafe area. The main door to the club had an eye-level window, approximately 6"x 6", covered by a wire mesh. The mesh was rusted and not well secured; it would be easy to push it out. Inside the club, the small window on the door had a cover with a latch, which could be opened to see who was on the other side.

Inside the 20'x20' room that served as the club everything was old, dusty and worn. There were a dozen or so mismatched tables with equally mismatched chairs, each salvaged from what others had discarded over the years. The fluorescent lighting was dim; some bulbs worked, others didn't. Surprisingly, the water ran clear in the rusted sink next to the small toilet that in the bathroom.

"So, what kind of party do you want to have?" asked Pablo, "Danny mentioned, it's for Lola."

"Just some friends, mostly Lola's, since she's the one going away."

"And she got her GED," Crystal added. "We just want to play some music and have a little food."

"Is there going to be any drinking? I don't want a bunch of kids getting drunk and puking all over my place," Pablo said. "I don't serve anybody underage."

Lola couldn't hide her distaste for Pablo or his club, "Would anyone notice a difference in this place if someone did throw up? You can control who gets served and how much they drink. We just want some beer, anyway. Charge us at the end of the party."

You can smoke a little weed and even enjoy a bit of coke... as long as there is enough for me," he smiled.

Lola asked quietly, "Do you know anyone who can get us some coke?"

Danny, who had been listening to the conversation, spoke up, "I know where we can get some coke for a real good price."

Pablo turned to his son, "And just who is this drug connection, hijo?"

"He's a super in a high-rise building near Montefiore Hospital. I can drive us there since I am the only one here with a car."

Danny threw this dig at his father; Pablo didn't have his own car. He had to use his son's when he needed one.

"I will come with you three to make sure you don't get into trouble," Pablo smirked, "and to make sure you don't get ripped off."

It never occurred to anyone that the girls should not be going along with this.

They piled into Danny's beat up yellow Oldsmobile Cutlass, the girls in the back.

Danny found a parking space on the street right in front of the building. The super's apartment was in the basement of an old building at the end of a small alley. Pablo, Lola and Crystal followed Danny, now acting like the man in charge, to the entrance door.

A loud voice answered Danny's knock, "*¿Quién esté ahi?*"

"*Es Danny.*"

The door opened a crack. The super, Ernesto Malino, known as *Cubano*, filled the opening with his enormous frame and peered at the group.

Lola and Crystal looked at each other with concern. They knew they had made a serious mistake.

Cubano came to the United States as one of thousands of criminals during the *Mariel Sealift*. The United States, in efforts to help Cubans flee their homeland during the Carter Administration, was later sharply criticized as it became known that Cuba had also released prisoners and mental health patients into the stream of emigrants. In Cuba, Cubano was known as an *enforcer*, a murderer. Cubano proudly wore the badge of his specialty in a small tattoo in the web of his right hand, between his thumb and forefinger.

Cubano did not seem happy to see the group at his door but reluctantly invited them in.

"What do you want, Danny? And who is this old man?"

"He is my *papa*, and the girls need a favor."

Danny, too, realized the mistake of bringing the two girls.

Once inside, Lola and Crystal became even more uneasy, not only because of Cubano's filthy appearance and gruff demeanor, but also because of the presence of two additional older men. Enrique Diaz, aka *Tramposo* and Bernardo Lopez, aka *Vato*, looked to be in their late 20's. They, too, were hard looking men, unwelcoming to Danny, Pablo and the girls.

Cubano's apartment was dirty and dark. The only two windows were covered by heavy curtains to block any light from entering.

Danny attempted to break the tension, "The girls are having a small party in my papa's club and wished to buy a small amount of coke, Amigo."

"What kind of party?"

"Lola is going into the Army; it's a going-away party," Danny offered.

"Sit here," Cubano instructed the girls, pointing to two mismatched, soiled armchairs. Each girl began to read the fear on the other's face.

"When are you going into the Army, Chica?"

Barely audible, Lola answered, "at the end of this month."

Cubano snatched the small purse from Lola's hand and rifled through the contents, looking for identification. Upon seeing the letters P.D. on a small notebook, he yelled, you some kind of narc, Chica?" He sneered with unarguable belief in his assumption.

The air was sucked from the room.

Cubano was enraged. "Are you here to arrest me, you fucking bitch cop? His fury seemed, to the girls, to double his size.

Lola spoke quietly in Spanish to try to calm the man, "Yo no soy un policía." Cubano refused to turn his intent look from Crystal, who had somehow captured his attention.

"I am not a police officer," Lola said in English.

Cubano pulled Enrique and Bernardo, who had been watching the scene, into his rant. "Amigos, you think these two putas are here to rip me off?"

"Danny, tell Cubano we are not here to rip him off, "Lola pleaded, "We're not policía!"

But Danny just stood frozen against the wall.

Pablo, too, was paralyzed in fear. He was not going to be the target of Cubano's rage, well aware of the violent reputation of the Marietta from the Mariel Sealift.

Pablo stared at his son with a silent warning, *keep your mouth shut.*

Cubano raged, pointing a .38 at Crystal. "Tell me the truth you lying bitch or I will put a bullet in this little puta's head."

Enrique and Bernardo pulled their guns and stared ruthlessly at Danny and Pablo. Bernardo smiled menacingly and caressed his Uzi as though it were a pet cat. He was not going to miss out on this unfolding action.

Cubano suddenly left the living room. For a brief moment there was a calm, everyone thought that he had cooled down. The four did a collective sigh of relief. The calm was short lived, the terror resumed when Cubano re-entered carrying a fist full of large green plastic garbage bags and a large spool of twine.

Lola carefully and slowly tried to stand. She thought she could find some way to calm things, to leave. But Cubano shouted, "You sit down and don't move, bitch."

"What are you going to do to us? Lola, what is he going to do to us?" Crystal asked, paralyzed with fear.

"Cubano, in his drug induced paranoia, was fully convinced that the two girls were undercover cops, he hissed, "You will soon find out, putas."

Bernardo stared at Crystal, anxious to shoot if she moved.

Cubano ripped the rope-like cord that had been holding one of the curtains back, brutally yanked Lola up from her chair, tightly bound her wrists behind her back. With another piece of rope, he tied her ankles tightly together, then shoved her back down onto the frayed seat.

Cubano looked at Lola, and laughed as she tried to plead with him to stop.

Lola screamed one last time as Cubano taped her mouth closed and hogtied her, pulling her hands close to her feet. He violently pushed the girl onto the plastic bag that was lying open on the floor.

Cubano turned to glare at Crystal, who was whimpering in terror, "You shut up or Bernardo will gladly shoot you." Bernardo took a step closer to Crystal, bent so that their eyes met, and smiled widely, baring his stained teeth and releasing his rancid breath.

Cubano turned his attention back to Lola. With one swift movement, Cubano pulled the bag up and over Lola and secured it tightly at the top. He added another rope on the outside of the bag, around her neck.

When Crystal screamed, Cubano smashed his fist down on her head with the force of a pile driver. Crystal slumped, unconscious.

Cubano turned his full attention back to the writhing form of Lola. He pressed his heavy foot against her back then pulled on the rope around her neck until the squirming stopped.

He then bagged Crystal's unconscious form in exactly the same way. He put a rope around her neck and pulled, to make sure she was dead.

Cubano, never one to take a chance, ordered the thugs, Vato and Tramposo, to put two more bags on the bodies "just in case," he sneered.

All the while, both Danny and Pablo stood watching, terrified to so much as blink, in fear for their own lives.

The two lifeless bodies in common trash bags were stacked in a heap in the center of one room. The place not only smelled like a garbage dump, it looked like one.

"You two pendejos created this mess and you are going to help clean it up." Cubano waved his gun back and forth in front of Pablo and Danny. He faced Danny, "Go out and pull your car to the front of the building."

Cubano turned to Bernardo, "Vato, go with this asshole and get your car close to the building as well. If he is stupid enough to try to run, shoot him." Cubano looked at Danny again, "If you try something stupid tu padre estáto muerto." Danny knew what Cubano was capable of and to disobey would be suicide.

Cubano ordered Pablo to haul the two bags out to the alley and dump them next to trash already piled there.

Pablo did as commanded, with Enrique on his heels, gun pulled and ready to shoot.

As the four men did as instructed, Cubano produced a small bag of cocaine, which he poured onto an old TV dinner tray. "Now I can have my shit without that cop bitch causing trouble."

The white line of cocaine disappeared up the killer's nose.

CHAPTER 8

Nightfall and darkness came quickly. The temperature was dropping and snow mixed with freezing rain steadily fell. The winter weather helped keep pedestrian activity to a minimum.

Cubano stood from his chair. "Time to go," he said to Pablo and Danny, signaling with his thumb toward the door.

Once outside, Bernardo, Enrique and Cubano stood beside the two cars. Bernardo had his Uzi ready for any trouble; Enrique, his Smith & Wesson 9mm.

Cubano motioned to Danny and Pablo to get the bags and dump them, one into each car trunk.

Cubano directed Enrique to ride with Danny in his old, beat-up Cutlass. He and Pablo would be in Bernardo's blue 1980 Chevy Caprice, ironically an old police car.

"You stay close to our car and don't do anything stupid," Cubano told Danny. "You make a mistake and Tramposo will shoot you, I will shoot your stupid father. Then we will have four assholes to dump. Now let's get these two putas out of the Bronx."

The caravan traveled north on the Bronx River Parkway until it reached the Hutchinson River Parkway.

"Take this road north," Cubano pointed to the entrance to the Hutch.

"Follow him *Amigo,* I don't know where Cubano is planning to go, but we will follow." Obeying Enrique's orders, Danny's car fell in behind Bernardo's.

The further north they travelled, the worse the weather

became. Cubano made a decision to turn off the highway. "I don't trust that estúpido Danny to know how to drive in this weather. We are far enough out of the Bronx now."

They turned onto Lincoln Road, by the entrance to Lakeside High School. Bernardo was barely getting traction from his bald tires on the icy road.

"Stop the car here," Cubano ordered.

"Vato, Tramposo, you keep a close eye. Someone stops to ask questions shoot them."

"What if they are cops?"

"*Especially* if they are cops."

The men got out of the cars. Cubano pointed at Danny and Pablo, "You two assholes get the bags out of the trunks and throw them over the guard rail onto the piles of leaves over there. Then let's get outta here."

The leaves and the bags were quietly covered by a light blanket of snow.

CHAPTER 9

Friday, March 9th

I arrived at work early Friday morning, anxious to get started on the biggest case of my young career.

I was going over some of the photos when Lieutenant Capanno came into the squad room. "Rocco, I need to see you in my office."

The lieutenant didn't look particularly happy. He leaned forward with his elbows on his desk and his face cradled in his hands, "Close the door. Rocco, you know I have a great deal of confidence and respect for your abilities, which is why I gave you this case."

I cut the lieutenant off mid-sentence, "I hear a big BUT coming."

Capanno said, "I just came from the chief's office."

"He doesn't think I can do it?" I asked, feeling disappointment start to take over.

"No, it's not that. You are staying on the case. As far as I'm concerned, it's *your* case! The chief wants me to assign a detective with you, though. He says because you are still a patrolman, if we don't have a bona fide detective on the case, he's sure to get shit from the rest of the squad."

"I understand." I said, relieved.

The case was still mine, but I worried that the chief thought I couldn't do it without a detective, despite reassurance from Lieutenant Capanno.

You'll be working with Detective Glen Smith," he said.

"Who? Smitty?"

"Yeah, Smitty. Your schedules already overlap a few days."

"My God Lieu, does the chief really think he can do a better job than I can? I couldn't get past feeling slighted. And I was annoyed; I didn't like Smitty's shitty personality or his quirky way of speaking, using *gr* instead of *dr*, like *griving* instead of *driving*.

I chuckled. "The Medical Examiner's assessment is that at least one of our victims was Hispanic, can you imagine how Smitty might pronounce Latino names?"

Then Capanno started laughing. "This is certainly not the kind of case for that. I know he's a colorful person and his demeanor is less than, shall we say, *diplomatic*." Capanno became serious, "Look, I'll make sure your shifts are not identical so you'll get a break from him."

More seriously he added, "Get ready for your first autopsy experience, Kid. And Rocco, I know that Smitty will put as much of the work off on you as possible..." The lieutenant sat back in his chair, sipped some coffee and continued, "...and I'm counting on that. Don't let him do anything alone that you won't be able to attest to in court. Do you understand me? I mean *anything*."

"I got you," I nodded.

"I can't wait for him to retire," he said. "You guys are going to the M.E.'s office today to observe the autopsies of our victims." Capanno sighed, "Don't let him screw this up."

Detective Smith arrived at work, fifteen minutes late, having stopped for breakfast. Smitty usually wore a trench coat over a colorful, often wrinkled, sports jacket.

I decided to get this partnership off with a little light sarcasm. "Hey, Glen, how come your jacket is so wrinkled?"

He looked down at his coat, "My wife washed it with the *grapes*."

"Grapes?"

"Yeah, the things in front of the windows."

I just laughed. There it was...*grapes* instead of *drapes*.

With more friendliness and a need to get things moving I said, "You and I are going to be together on this case. Our first thing will be the autopsies today."

"You're in luck, Kid. Stick with me and you might learn something."

I turned back to see Lieutenant Capanno seeing him shaking his head. I swear I heard him laughing.

CHAPTER 10

S mitty parked the unmarked police car in a space marked *Medical Examiner Personnel Only*. Rules were not for him.

We entered the morgue through a rear door, adjacent to the parking lot. Once inside, Smitty wandered away; I assumed looking for something to eat.

I made my way down the dimly lit corridor of the County morgue. The place was more than showing its age. There were plans for a new laboratory facility which would house the morgue, but that wouldn't happen for a while. The current facility was adequate. The wear and tear on the pea-green tiled walls and grey tiled floor made the otherwise clean facility look less than sterile.

Chief Medical Examiner Dr. James Lowman was nearing retirement and his years of accomplishments were well documented by the plaques and commendations that hung on the walls of his office.

Dr. Lowman was sitting at his desk going through paperwork. He looked up as I entered. "I'll be performing these two autopsies. I hope these will be the last I have to perform on such young victims. Who's the lead detective on this case?"

Out of respect for the position I said, "Detective Smith."

Lowman shook his head in dismay. "Oh my God, hasn't he retired yet? Where is he? Looking for something to eat?"

"He's in the building, I am sure Detective Smith is anxious to learn what happened to these two women."

"You ever watch an autopsy before?" Lowman asked.

"No, these will be my first."

I explained to Dr. Lowman that although this would be my first post- mortem examination, it was not my first experience with dead bodies. I had been at other homicide scenes and suicides. I saw piles of burned corpses in front of blocked exit doors at the scene of the hotel fire in 1980.

As if he had been informed of the moniker given to me in the Detective Bureau, he said, "You'll do fine, Kid, just keep your hands in your pockets and your eyes open." Dr. Lowman stood up from his desk. "Let's get going, I'm sure Detective Smith will find his way to the tables."

I followed Dr. Lowman into the autopsy room. The room was as old and weathered-looking as the hallways. The walls were tiled the same pea-green; the floor stained terrazzo. Bright light came from circular fixtures hung from the ceiling. The lights were brightest over the stainless-steel autopsy tables. The room resembled a large hospital operating room.

The smell upon entering was an assault. I had never experienced anything like it before. My eyes teared from the sting of the formaldehyde. I marveled that anyone could get used to it.

The bags containing the bodies were placed on individual cold, stainless-steel tables.

"Take as many photos as you want to while the girls are still dressed, but once the autopsies start, our photographer takes over." Dr. Lowman raised his eyes to meet mine, "We will make sure you and Detective Smith have copies of our pictures; they can be used for your investigation."

I readied my camera and took my place alongside Dr. Lowman as he prepared to open the first bag. Dr. Lowman went about his work with no show of emotion.

"I know you want to document as much as possible so I will proceed slowly. I will describe each procedure, not only for your benefit, but also for the audio documentation. Later, the audio will be transcribed."

The doctor carefully removed each of the three trash bags tied over the bodies; he kept the bags as intact as possible, mindful of the likelihood of the trace evidence that would be on the plastic. As each bag was removed, it was wrapped in plain brown paper by Lowman's assistant and marked as evidence with the M.E. case number. Case numbers represented the department of, Medical Examiner of Westchester, year and subject number.

Dr. Lowman began the audio, "Each body is covered with three bags secured with twine; the bags appear to be industrial-strength. The multiple bags were pulled over the bodies from opposite directions. The bag closest to each body was placed with the victim's feet at the bottom; the second, from the head downward, the third with the victim's feet in first."

The removal of the bags seemed painstakingly slow.

When all the bags had been removed, I saw the bound body of 84-ME-560 later identified as Lola Vasquez.

"From this point on," said Dr. Lowman, "I refer to the victims by case number for documentation and for cross-referencing any evidence discovered."

At that moment, I thought about my own two young daughters, Marie and Patrice, and what it would feel like to see one of them on this table, referred to as a number. The thought was horrifying.

Lowman's instructions brought me back to the reality in front of me. "Make sure you have enough film for the next procedure, removal of the ropes. I'll give you time to document each step; I'll point out details you should focus on. Start with the condition and position of the ropes. Get some close-ups of the knot patterns and position of the ropes on the different body parts."

"Thank you, doctor. The new color slide film only has eight exposures per roll, so I'll need to keep reloading the camera."

"Not a problem, officer, these girls are not going anywhere."

I wasn't sure if Dr. Lowman was always this helpful or if

his helpfulness was in consideration of the fact that this was my first autopsy. Once he started to remove the rope, I understood why I would need to take so many pictures.

Dr. Lowman continued my education, "I am tying a string to each side of the rope where I will cut; this will enable reconstruction and will not disturb the knots. You will also be able to see where our cuts were made so they won't be confused with cuts made by the person who tied them."

The first piece of cord that Lowman removed was from the wrists of the first body. He waited for me to take a close-up photo of the way it was tied, the cord was approximately twelve inches long, with a loop the size of an avocado at each end. I didn't realize at the time how *important* this detail was going to be to the investigation.

Dr. Lowman then meticulously removed the remaining ropes from the body until all were removed and the body could be straightened. This was not easy: the bodies had been shoved into bags in a fetal position and rigor mortis had set in.

As with the bags, the piece of rope was identified with an evidence tag bearing the M.E. number assigned to the first body. Each step was patiently repeated with the second bag holding the body of the girl who would later be identified as Crystal Ramos. As each bag was opened and the body of a young girl became visible, a slightly bloated but still pretty face of a dead girl was revealed.

"I am going to remove the clothing now," Dr. Lowman said. "You will wait in the evidence room and we will have the clothes brought in. You can examine and photograph them there. After we prepare the bodies for autopsy, you can come back in here, if you wish; however, you will not be allowed to take photographs."

"Thank you," I said, "I'll be there."

Grateful for a break, I took this opportunity to go to the rest room to wash my face, hoping to rid the stench of the formaldehyde and what other strange odors that seemed to be sticking to me. The soap had a strong, flowery fragrance. I put some on my finger tips and pushed the soap up my nose. Thankfully, it masked the stench of death. Leaving the restroom, I wondered what happened to Detective Smith. Where the hell was he?

I found him in the evidence room. Smitty was rifling through the clothing that had been just been brought in. He looked like someone at a rummage sale.

"Glen, what the hell are you doing? This is evidence."

"Calm down, Kid, we are going to get this stuff from the M.E. sooner or later."

To stop Detective Smith from possibly destroying any evidentiary value of the clothing I said, "We need to lay them out on the table as they would have been on the victims so I can photograph them. This may help with identification."

The body from the first bag was later identified as Lola Vasquez. While laying her clothes out, I felt something in the top front pocket of the jeans; I withdrew two loose keys. In addition to laying the keys on a piece of paper and carefully photographing them, I traced them and duplicated the engraved identifying marks. One was a brass key that looked like a typical door lock or deadbolt key; it had a series of numbers punched into its rounded top. The other key was silver; it, too, looked like a door key, but had no identifying marks other than the manufacturer's name.

After photographing "Lola's" clothes, I went on to "Crystal's," still 84-ME-561. The case numbers referred to the number of autopsies performed to date this year. It was only March.

Aside from the two keys, neither girl had anything on them or with them that would assist in identification. Nothing of Lola's clothing seemed especially unique: waist-length black leather jacket, bright pink blouse, blue jeans, white socks, mid-calf black leather boots, light blue panties, and no bra. Crystal's clothing, although nothing special, did have some distinctive features. Her sweater had knit sleeves and a fleece lambskin vest. Her pants were brown with white stripes, a white blouse, white socks, dirty white Puma sneakers, and white panties, no bra.

After photographing the clothes of the girls and carefully placing them back in their respective paper wrappers, I was advised that the autopsies were about to begin. "Are you coming, Glen?"

"No, I've seen enough of those damn things."

CHAPTER 11

With nervous trepidation and liquid soap in each nostril, I approached the stainless-steel table on which lay the lifeless body of 84-ME-560.

The cold autopsy table has raised edges and resembles an enormous baking sheet. Faucets and drains line the sides to wash away body fluids.

Lola's body was in a supine position, almost as if she were sleeping. Her eyes were closed and her mouth open, as if trying to speak. She would have to let the examination of her lifeless body provide the clues that would solve the mystery of her death.

Dr. Lowman began his visual examination and recorded his findings, "Number 560 bears no cuts, gunshot holes, scars, or tattoos."

The examination resulted in more of what wasn't present than what was. There were no wounds from sharp objects such as knives, nor were there any gunshot wounds. Lola had no tattoos, and the lack of any scars suggested that until her untimely death, she had not suffered any serious injuries or surgeries. Lola's body was measured and weighed by a lab technician.

"Five feet, four inches, one hundred five pounds."

"M.E. 560 has shoulder-length brown hair and brown eyes," Dr. Lowman spoke into the microphone mounted above the procedure table.

Listening intently and writing the doctor's findings in my own notebook, I asked if I could interrupt with questions as he proceeded.

Without looking up, Lowman answered, "Yes. Keep them related to the point of the examination I am performing."

A body block was placed beneath Lola's back to push her chest forward, allowing arms and neck to fall back. The body block makes it easier to cut the chest open.

The external examination completed, it was time for the internal exam.

The doctor's narration continued, "To open the chest cavity, I will make a "Y" incision starting at the left shoulder and continuing to the center of the breastbone; a second incision will extend from the right shoulder to the first incision at the breastbone. An incision from the bottom of this "V" to the pubic bone will allow the chest cavity and majority of internal organs to be exposed."

Using a scalpel, Dr. Lowman peeled back the skin, muscle and soft tissue. The chest flap, starting at the bottom of the "V" portion of the "Y" cut, was pulled over Lola's face, exposing her rib cage and throat. The effectiveness of my smell-masking liquid soap was quickly wearing off. As much as I imagined that the sight of an autopsy might bother me, it was the smell that was most sickening.

"Is that what the insides of a body usually look like, Doc?" They appeared to be green.

"The color and odor are indications of how long the body was dead. Decomposition intensifies the smell," the doctor glanced at me with a smile, "which I see you are trying to mask with the soap on the tips of your fingers."

"I am going to cut the ribs and remove the breast bone." Lowman picked up a tool that resembled a bolt cutter. "With the breast bone removed, I can spread the chest cavity to expose the subject's organs."

"I will begin the organ removal with the esophagus and larynx. Next, I will sever the remaining organs from the spine to remove them intact. These organs will later be dissected and examined more closely. The stomach is carefully examined to allow analysis of its contents," Dr. Lowman explained, then looked at me. "This portion of the autopsy is completed. Why don't you take a break before we start on the second victim."

I was grateful for the reprieve. I returned to the restroom where again I tried to wash away some of the stink and replenish my nostrils with soap. I remembered that I had left Smitty in the evidence room and wondered what he might be doing. I also remembered what Lieutenant Capanno said. "Don't leave Smitty alone..."

"Got your soap?" Dr. Lowman asked with a chuckle when I re-entered the autopsy room.

Dr. Lowman performed the same careful procedure with Crystal, 84-ME-561, as he had with Lola. Crystal's height was measured as 5 feet 1 inch, her weight, only 86 lbs. She had short, black curly hair and brown eyes. Crystal had no tattoos; she did have a scar on her lower abdomen and another on her left shoulder. The reasons for these scars which were old, was not immediately apparent.

There were no stab or gunshot wounds. There was, however, one distinguishing find on top of Crystal's head.

Dr. Lowman stated, "There is an indication that number 561 may have received an injury to the top of her head; this is reason to carefully examine the brain once it is removed." The purpose of the additional examination would help determine if the injury contributed to cause of death.

Dr. Lowman removed the body block from Crystal's back and placed it like a cradle under her neck to raise her head and enable access to the brain. He took a scalpel and made cuts to the scalp which resulted in a flap of skin over her face and a flap to the rear, over the back of her neck, thus exposing the skull.

Dr. Lowman started his electric saw; it looked like a large

electric tooth brush with a sharp circular blade where the brush would be. The whirring noise of the saw indicated the high rotation of the blade, necessary for neatly cutting through the bone. With great precision, the doctor made a cut around the circumference of the skull, creating a "skull cap" of sorts.

Dr. Lowman pried the skull cap loose and removed it. The soft tissue membrane covering the brain created a sound similar to that of a large suction cup being pried from a drain when the skull cap was pulled free.

"Now that the skull cap is off, I can remove the brain and place it in the tray for weight."

The tray hanging at the bottom of a scale is similar to the one which was used by the neighborhood fish monger I remembered seeing as a kid. Lowman would later examine the brain for evidence of trauma or other possible cause for the injury.

It was time to find Smitty and head back to the office.

CHAPTER 12

"**O**pen your window, Kid, you stink." Smitty was not prone to niceties. As we pulled onto the highway he said, "You should have put a *grop* of menthol rubbing cream up your nose; that stuff masks all the dead-body odors."

Shaking my head, with a slight chuckle I whispered, "*Grop* for *drop.*" Thankfully Smitty didn't hear me.

"*Now* you tell me this? It would have been a helpful bit of information to have before spending hours in the autopsy room."

Tired from mental and emotional exhaustion after the hours spent at the two autopsies, I failed to notice a box sitting on the back seat of our unmarked car until Smitty took it and carried it into the squad room when we returned.

"What's that?" Lieutenant Capanno asked Detective Smith.

"It's the clothes the M.E. took off the two stiffs."

"He gave that to you?" Capanno questioned.

"No, but I figured we were gonna get it sooner or later. Why wait for later?"

Capanno turned to me. "Rocco, come into my office please."

I knew this was not going to be pleasant. I remembered full well the warning not to leave Glen alone.

"Did you know that moron took the clothes?"

"No, I assumed the M.E. gave the clothes to him." I knew full well he didn't. I didn't want to throw Detective Smith under the bus.

"Go home Kid, you had a full day. You can do your reports on today's activity tomorrow."

"Tomorrow is Saturday, Lieu, you want me in?"

"Come in for a couple of hour's overtime to write up your report and make sure the stuff Smith brought in is properly tagged and packaged."

It didn't take a seasoned detective to figure out the lieutenant was not happy with what Detective Smith had done.

Once back in my own car, I opened all the windows even though it was a cold March day. I put the air conditioner on in hopes of keeping the awful stench from stinking up my Camaro.

I entered my house through the garage and took off all my clothes in the basement. I threw what was washable into the washing machine and left my trousers, which had to go to the dry cleaners, in the garage. I then went upstairs and got right into the shower.

Audrey called, "Rocco, are you OK?"

Audrey and I had been married for thirteen years. I was lucky to have a wife who was supportive and understanding of my job.

"I need to freshen up," I answered her. "Then I'll tell you about my day."

It took a while, but I finally felt a bit cleaner and could barely notice the smell. I went into the bedroom and put on a clean shirt and a clean pair of pants. I was now able to face Audrey.

"Are you OK?" she asked again. "I know this was your first autopsy."

"I knew it would be visibly disturbing, but the worst part turned out to be the smell. I don't know how these M.E. people work in that place every day."

"Are you ready for some dinner?"

"Surprisingly, I am hungry."

"I made pizza, is the sight of sauce going to bother you?"

I said pizza was just fine and enjoyed my dinner. I was happy to have a different smell to inhale.

CHAPTER 13

Saturday, March 10th

Saturday morning, I woke up after a restless sleep. The visions of the autopsy procedures were still fresh in my mind as was the fear that the smell would never really disappear. My daughters were already up and arguing. Hearing them was reassuring: they were alive and well.

I seldom worried about my daughters fighting or arguing; I was the eldest of three brothers and one sister in a vocal Italian family. That type of interaction was an almost daily occurrence. Audrey, however, did not handle their squabbles well. Audrey was an only child and couldn't understand how almost incessant arguing could be normal sibling behavior.

"That's my mug and you know it is," Marie made a grab for the ceramic mug.

Patrice snapped back, "So the princess can't drink out of any other cup?"

They stopped their fighting when I came into the kitchen. Audrey had told them that I had been through a hellish experience so they were being kind to Dad. Whenever my shift allowed me to see them in the morning, I would give each daughter a good morning kiss; today I threw in a hug to go with the kiss.

Audrey brought me a cup of coffee. "Stop obsessing," she whispered after I asked her to take a whiff and let me know if I smelled...like death. "That smell is just in your mind. Trust me, if you reeked, I would tell you." Then she winked, "I would have made you sleep in your car."

That put a smile on my face, at least for a short while.

She sipped her tea, "I'm glad you didn't faint and keel over like the cops do in the opening of *Quincy*."

"Leave it to you to find the positive. You're right, at least I did stay upright." I finished my coffee and orange juice, failing to muster an appetite with the images of the autopsies crowding my senses.

Since this was an off day for me and I was just going to be writing reports on an overtime basis, there was no reason to dress up for work. I put on a pair of jeans and a sweatshirt. I told Audrey I wouldn't be at headquarters too long. When I got into my car, I was relieved that there were no remnants of the smell from yesterday; however, leaving the windows open again seemed like a good idea.

I checked in with the desk sergeant at 9AM. "Hi, Sarge. The lieutenant told me to come in for a couple of hours to write up my reports on yesterday's activities."

Sarge looked up from his paperwork, "OK, Rocco, I'll put you on the work sheet; let me know when you're leaving."

I was alone in the division office; the duty detective, Andy Scollari, had not yet arrived. Because it was Saturday and Lieutenant Capanno probably wouldn't be there, Detective Scollari was in no rush to show up. I liked Andy. He tended to be friendly, perhaps because we were both Italian. Or perhaps it was his outgoing personality that made him likeable.

I decided to process all of the film I had taken in addition to writing my reports, since I had the uninterrupted time to do it. I knew that if I tried to develop the photos during my normal tour, I would be interrupted by the situations that always came up unexpectedly. I still had the two burglaries to work on as well. Even though I had this major case assigned to me, I was still responsible for any other cases that came up during my tour. In smaller police departments like ours, investigators investigated all types of crimes, assaults, robbery, burglaries and homicides."

I took out my memo pad and began typing my "supplemental" report. Anything written and attached to the original case report would have the same case number and would be considered supplemental. I wanted my report to be thorough, which would take extra time: my two-finger hunt and peck typing left a lot to be desired.

My memo notes were meticulously annotated with dates and times so that the chronology and correlation of the reports to the events was correct. After about an hour, my supplementals were completed and ready to be placed in the lieutenant's inbox for review. I was suddenly in the mood for a bagel.

I called the desk sergeant. "Sarge, I'm going down to the deli to get a coffee and a bagel. You want anything?"

At some point during my typing frenzy, Detective Scollari had come in. When he heard my offer to the desk sergeant he said, "That sounds good, Rocco. I'll take a coffee and buttered bagel, too."

I looked around to see Andy at his desk. "When did you get here?"

"I've been here for a while but I didn't want to interrupt your typing, if that's what you call it."

"OK to take the detective car?" I asked.

"Sure, go ahead," he grinned, "but don't waste time. I'm hungry."

In addition to wanting something to eat, I needed some cold March air to clear my head after reliving the gory details of the autopsies for my report. Lieutenant Capanno was showing a great deal of confidence in my investigative abilities, so I wanted to make sure my work lived up to his expectations. Lieutenant Capanno had been a mentor to me from the time I came on the job. We had grown to have mutual respect.

While in the downtown delicatessen, I saw Lieutenant Doore, the shift commander for the day tour.

"What are you doing here today, Kid? Isn't it your day off?"

"The lieutenant told me to come in and write up some of my reports and develop the film from yesterday."

"It's pretty obvious those girls were not from Lakeside, so why spend all this time on it?" He added, as if looking into his crystal ball of investigative outcomes, "You'll never find out who they were or who killed them anyway."

I liked Lieutenant Doore as a person, but had no regard for his idea of what a police officer should or should not do. I took the high road and said, "Just doing my job, Lieutenant."

I got the coffees and bagels and left the deli before I had to listen to any more of Lieutenant Doore's predictions.

I returned to headquarters, gave the desk sergeant and desk assistant their coffees, and went back into the detective division. Andy was still at his desk waiting for his coffee and bagel. I decided not to relate my conversation with Lieutenant Doore to Andy; I didn't know what kind of relationship they shared.

Andy smiled, "You gonna do some more typing now that your two fingers had a break?"

"No, I think the typewriter needs the break. I'm going to process the film. Do you want to see how this new film gets processed?"

Andy shrugged his shoulders, "Sure, why not?"

I knew Andy preferred not to use the 35mm camera, so his interest in the process caught me a little off guard.

I was careful to read the instructions a couple of times before beginning the development process. If I screwed up the film, there would be no way to recreate the events and the confidence Lieutenant Capanno had shown would be history. The process went as smoothly as my first attempt had when shooting the test rolls and the ones I had developed at the crime scene. Roll after roll of the color slide film was now properly developed.

"That doesn't look too complicated, Rocco." Andy said. "It would be good to develop color here."

"This is the only color we can do here, Andy. The other color 35mm film still has to be sent out."

For the purpose of continuity of evidence control and confidentiality, sending film to an outside vendor for processing is not a preferred practice.

After processing each roll of film, I used the slide cutter and slide frames to produce individual slides. Each slide was numbered and corresponded to a photo log created to document the details of each photo. The photo log had information such as photo number, subject, camera, lens setting, flash use, date, time, and corresponding evidence number. Film prints would have all the same information on a photo information form placed or stamped on the backside of the print.

I took the slide projector into the interrogation room and shut the light to project each slide onto the rear white wall in the room. Projecting the slides enhanced observation of the details in each photo.

"Wow! I am impressed," Andy said, "They look great. Color is always effective in court."

I wasn't sure if this made Andy a convert to the 35mm camera, but I was willing to settle for his approval.

I carefully placed each slide in the slots of a plastic slide holder sheet. Each slide holder sheet holds 20 slides; I found I was quickly filling the sheets and made a note to myself to get more. I inserted the slides in sequential order. I attached the sheet to my supplemental report on the film processing, along with the photo log and placed everything in Lieutenant Capanno's inbox for review. I stopped at the front desk to let the desk sergeant know I was finished for the day.

"Done for the day?" The sergeant asked.

"Yeah, I will try to enjoy what's left of my weekend."

I was ready to go home and relax before returning Monday morning, for the next phase of the investigation to begin, the identification of the two bodies.

I was determined to identify the victims and had an added incentive: prove Lieutenant Doore wrong in his prediction of failure.

CHAPTER 14

Sunday, March 11th

On Sunday morning, I sat at the kitchen table cutting articles about the case out of the local newspaper. It was a big case for me and I wanted to memorialize as much of it as possible.

The headline on the first article from Friday's local paper read, FROZEN BODIES OF 2 WOMEN IN GARBAGE BAGS DISCOVERED ACROSS FROM LAKESIDE HIGH SCHOOL. The article was brief. There wasn't much information other than the discovery of and sketchy description of the crime scene, it read; *The bound, frozen bodies of two unidentified women, possibly teen-agers, were found Thursday in plastic bags near Lakeview High School. Both were fully clothed wearing jeans and shirts, but neither carried identification.*

Lieutenant Capanno had made it clear from the onset of the investigation that any news releases would come from him. He would control the information going out. Limiting the source of news is an excellent policy. Some officers who speak to the media, even with good intentions, tend to leak sensitive information that could impact the investigation. There is also, no shortage of people who admit to crimes and activities that they were not involved in. The more detailed information made public, the easier it is for them to seem credible. Lieutenant Capanno was careful not to mention the names of the investigators, thereby reducing the opportunity for media personnel to attempt to bypass the department's official source and contact individual officers.

Saturday's news article, DEATHS OF 2 FROZEN WOMEN STILL A MYSTERY. *Autopsies gave no clue to the cause of death of two unidentified women whose frozen and bound bodies were found stuffed into plastic bags Thursday in Lakeside.* The autopsies did not reveal a definitive cause of death. What did not cause the deaths was covered: the girls were not shot, stabbed or beaten. *Initial tests also indicated the women had not been sexually abused. The women appeared to be teen-agers who had been dead for several days.*

As I was moving into the Sunday paper, the phone rang.

"Hon, it's your lieutenant," Audrey said.

"Hi Lieu, I was just reading the Sunday coverage of the crime." LINK TO THE BRONX PROBED IN 2 GIRLS' DEATHS. *Capanno said Saturday that an item found in one of the bags was the clue that led police to turn to police in the Bronx for help in search of some pieces in the puzzling case.*

"Their article mentioned a link to the Bronx Lieu. Where did this come from?"

"Those keys you found in the victim's pocket. Turned out one of the keys, the one with an identifying number stamped on it, was made at a store on Southern Boulevard, Tremont section of the Bronx. This may be a big break for us. I'm glad you were at the lab, Kid, 'cause Smitty would have either missed the keys or lost them."

I chuckled, but again, didn't disparage Detective Smith, after all, I had to work with him.

"I intentionally left out the information about the keys when I spoke to the press," Capanno said. "We still don't know if they belonged to the victims or to whoever killed them. That's why the article simply states a possible link."

"I got the photos from the M.E." Capanno continued, "I want you to compose some informational flyers to distribute to other law enforcement agencies that may be able to help us.

I've got some of our other detectives following up on any leads the press may have generated. So far, the few leads we got over the last couple of days have produced *nada*." Capanno paused, "Our primary focus has to be identification of our two victims."

I had my own theory about where the girls might have been from, or not from, due to the lack of any public outcry. Lakeside parents would have reported a missing girl to us right away. Also, our town had three college campuses, we would have heard if students were missing. I had to agree with Lieutenant Doore that the girls were definitely not from Lakeside. The close proximity of the crime scene to New York City and Connecticut, along with the proximity to the Hutch and I-95, added to the likelihood that the girls were not local. The victims could be from anywhere; we needed to get some credible leads.

I had a friend who was an artist. Often, his renderings appeared in the local newspaper in lieu of photographs that were too disturbing for public display or in place of detailed, officially documented evidence.

I contacted Gus Rizzo and asked him to meet me at police headquarters to work on sketches of the two victims. I needed to ask Capanno if he wanted the images released to the public.

I called Lieutenant Capanno to advise him of my plan. He liked the idea of having sketches to release to the press. "The victims are someone's daughters," he said. "I don't want their parents to see police photographs of their dead bodies."

CHAPTER 15

S o much for a quiet, relaxing Sunday at home. I was going back to the office to meet Gus and get started on the drawings.

When I got to headquarters, I checked in with Sergeant Edwards, the desk sergeant. "You're on the worksheet, Kid. Lieutenant Capanno is already in and he told me you'd be in, too."

Sergeant Edwards was one of the old-timers who I sincerely enjoyed. He told me that he believed I would do well and that he expected me to go places. He was one of the few people who I didn't mind calling me *Kid*.

I smiled when I walked further inside the office. There stood Lieutenant Capanno, impeccably dressed as always. I didn't want him to think I found anything about this case amusing, so I quickly hid the smile of appreciation of his predictable style...

"These are the pictures the M.E. sent us," Capanno said, wasting no time.

Even though they were black and white photographs, they brought the images of what I had witnessed during their autopsies back in vivid color. I could swear the smell from the autopsies permeated the photos.

"Is it me, Lieu, or do these things smell like dead bodies?"

He nodded knowingly, "I'm sure that's a smell you won't soon forget. It seems to stick to everything."

We went over the photos to determine which could be used in the informational flyers and which images needed to be modified in a sketch by Gus. Despite the Bronx connection, the police still had to work with the theory that the girls could have been from anywhere and that the keys may have belonged to the killer or killers. For this reason, getting a picture of the girls in the newspaper was essential to our investigation. Pictures sometimes jog a person's memory or recognition when written descriptions don't.

The lieutenant was attempting to make copies of the face head-shots we had gotten from the M.E. He was frustrated with the lack of detail in the reproductions.

Holding a copy of the photos in his hands, Capanno said, "Look how shitty these pictures look. This copy machine sucks."

"It's not the copy machine, Lieu. Reproducing pictures with detail takes a more sophisticated procedure."

"No Rocco, it's not the picture, it's this piece of shit machine," he insisted. Every time we try to copy pictures on it for something, they come out bad. You can't see any face detail and after we send them, things get worse when copies are made from our copies."

"Don't worry Lieu, it's a simple fix that can be done by half-toning the photos."

"Do what?" Capanno asked.

Rather than explain, I went over to Detective Roberts' desk and picked up the newspaper I knew would be there. I grabbed a magnifying glass and turned to a photo in the newspaper. "Look at the picture through the glass."

With the magnifying glass in hand, Capanno looked like Sherlock Holmes. "What am I looking for?"

"Dots. You are looking at the picture to see that it is made up of dots."

"OK, I see the dots. What does that mean?"

I handed one of the M.E.'s black and white pictures to him. "Look at this one. Do you see dots?"

"No, I don't."

"The dots are called half-tone and they help the reproduction maintain detail. When the one without half-tone is copied, all the detail is lost. If you were to examine a photograph in a magazine the dots would be smaller; smaller dots produce a higher quality picture."

Going back and forth with the magnifying glass from picture to newspaper, Capanno nodded and said, "I see the difference."

"I have a printer friend I can take these to. His copy will give us a much better-quality photo that will show detail. I'll stay with him while it's being done to maintain possession of all the copies and the printing plate."

He looked again at the photos. "I'd hate to think how much more difficult some aspects of this investigation would be if you didn't have so many friends."

"We'll see if they're still my friends after the favors."

Sergeant Edwards buzzed the lieutenant on the intercom to advise him that Gus Rizzo was at the front desk.

"Rocco, go out and greet Mr. Rizzo. Bring him back here."

Mr. Rizzo was an elegant man who looked much younger than his sixty-five years. His art was recognized worldwide and went well beyond newspaper reprints. Each week, I made it a point to look for Gus' by-line under newspaper drawings.

I brought him inside and introduced him to Lieutenant Capanno.

"I feel bad for taking you away from your family on a Sunday. We won't keep you too long," Capanno said, firmly shaking Gus' hand.

"I will try to help you," Rizzo said.

"Can you reproduce these to look like the girls as they did when they were alive?"

Rizzo nodded. "I'll have no problem sketching the women. Are the sketches needed for the information flyers you are going to make for distribution to other law enforcement agencies?" I had told Gus about my assignment.

"The sketches will be used for newspapers," Capanno said. "The morgue pictures will be used for the flyers. Here's a copy of each photo, Gus. Thank you so much for your help. We'll look forward to seeing your work as soon as possible. Now go home and enjoy your Sunday dinner."

Gus assured us that he would get his sketches to the reporter handling the case, Miss Johnson, before the end of the day. I thanked him sincerely and walked him out to his car. Then I headed back inside the office.

Deciding that I didn't want to drag another friend out of his home on a Sunday, I told the lieutenant that I'd visit my printer friend's shop first thing in the morning.

"Joe's shop is usually opened by 7AM. I'll have the flyers made before I come in." I sat down and began to compose the pertinent information that would supplement the photos. Each flyer would have to have as much information as possible to enable identification the victims.

I completed the flyer for Lola first:

IDENTIFICATION WANTED: HOMICIDE

Description: White (possible Hispanic) female, 5'4", 105 lbs., brown hair, brown eyes, believed to be more than 18 yrs.

Clothing: Last wearing black waist-length jacket, dark pink velour shirt, blue jeans, white socks, black leather calf-high boots.

Fingerprint: DI PI 17 DO PO 15 DO 15 DI 17
Class NCIC

Blood type: O Positive

Details: Body found bound and bagged alongside road-way; may have been dead 2 weeks prior to find on 03/08/84

Agency: Lakeside Police Department
210 South Avenue
Lakeside, New York 11467
Tel. 914 555-6000
Detective Division

Case: -I-84-3267 Victim 84-ME-560

Next was the flyer for Crystal:

IDENTIFICATION WANTED: HOMICIDE

Description: Black (possible Hispanic) female, 5'1", 86 lbs., black hair (large curls), brown eyes, age believed to be under 18 yrs.

Clothing: Last wearing sweater-type jacket (brown sleeves & collar) w/off white fleece-like body, off white knit blouse, maroon or brown Lee jeans with white stripes; white socks, white Puma sneakers.

Fingerprint: 02 tt aa 02 AA 01 03 tt tt 15
Class NCIC

Blood type: A Positive

Details: Body found bound and bagged alongside road-way, may have been dead 2 weeks prior to find on 03/08/84.

Agency: Lakeside Police Department
210 South Avenue
Lakeside, New York 11467
Tel. 914 555-6000
Detective Division

Case: -I-84-3267 Victim 84-ME-561

"Lieu," I said from my desk, "I'm finished with the information for the flyers. All that has to be done before printing is to add the higher quality photos. Anything else you need me for today?"

Lieutenant Capanno seemed pleased with the day's progress. "I think we got a lot done today. Tomorrow, I'm hoping we'll see Gus's sketches in the paper. I'm supposed to call Miss Johnson, to give her an update. I can't be too critical of her for pushing us for information; we do need their help in identifying these two girls. As soon as you come in tomorrow with the flyers, we'll get them out to as many agencies as we can. Make sure you print a sufficient number."

It was time to go home to enjoy what was left of my day off.

CHAPTER 16

Monday, March 12th

Monday morning began after a good night's sleep. I ate an early breakfast and then headed to Joe DiNapoli's print shop. My friend's shop was just around the corner from my house in Halsey, a quiet town close to Lakeside.

The printing presses were already cranking when I arrived.

"Hey, did you sleep here last night?" I asked.

Joe smiled. "You know I like to get an early start. Why are you so dressed up this morning?"

"I'm working plain clothes now. I have a favor to ask of you, Joe."

"I'm still into you for several favors before we get close to being even. Whatever you need, you got it."

I showed him the flyer originals and the two photos of the girls and explained that I needed high quality copies. The detail would be critical in the copies.

"The lieutenant was trying to do this on our copy machine, but the quality wasn't there. I told him you could fix that."

Joe was staring at the photos, shaking his head in disbelief, I continued, "I'll do most of the prep work to get the stats of the pictures entered and I'll make the plate for printing. I need you to run the press so that I don't wind up covered in ink." Running the press, I knew from experience, could be dirty work.

I had been in the graphic arts industry prior to becoming a

police officer. Since becoming an officer, I continued to work for Joe during my off hours, helping out making plates prior to printing.

I set up the vertical camera used to make film negatives or Photostats. "Joe, I want to use an 85 LPI."

The 85 lines-per-inch screen is used for newsprint; a 125 would look more like a magazine photo, but we weren't going for portrait quality. We needed just enough quality to avoid losing clarity when copied and recopied. I was sure the flyers would be photocopied by other police agencies.

I placed the photos on the lower copy board of the camera, placed the screen on the top glass and a piece of Photostat paper on top of the screen. The photos were trimmed and put onto the original information flyer sheets. Once the image was transferred to the metal plate, I rubbed it with two chemicals. I repeated this process for each flyer with a front face and profile photo of each girl.

"I'll need at least a hundred copies of each, Joe," I said, handing him the finished plates.

I made sure to collect every 'throw-away' copy, so that nothing would be left behind. "I'm going to take every sheet, Joe and I'm taking the plates, too. If we need any more copies, I'll bring them back."

I cleaned the ink off the plates and put them in the box with my flyers. "I really appreciate this."

"Anytime," he answered sincerely. "Good luck with the investigation."

I headed to headquarters with quality flyers, I knew Lieutenant Capanno would be appreciative.

CHAPTER 17

I entered headquarters, as I always did, through the front door. I didn't know if I would ever fall into the routine of using the back door as the other detectives usually did. Desk officers appreciated when detectives used the front door; it allowed them to know who was in. Desk sergeants are often seasoned officers who are at or over retirement age. They do not always get the respect they deserve, especially from the members of the detective division, who feel they have no need to account for their comings and goings.

I was surprised to see not only Lieutenant Capanno, but Detectives Scollari and Barney Burns. Neither detective was scheduled to work that morning. They were looking at the morning newspaper, which had run the sketches of the girls along with the article.

"We got a couple of calls because of the article," the lieutenant told me.

"From where, Lieu?"

"We got a call from someone in White Plains who claimed to have seen the girls. There were also a couple of calls from Connecticut."

The article mentioned the Bronx connection but noted the police were still unsure of where the girls were from. The sketches were excellent and portrayed a close likeness of each girl without the more gruesome detail of the original morgue pictures.

I showed the flyers to the lieutenant. He was pleased with the quality. "That's much better than I could get from the copy machine and to be honest, better than I thought they would look."

He continued, "Scollari and Burns are going to follow up the White Plains lead. You and I are going to follow the leads from Connecticut."

Every single lead had to be followed.

Detectives Burns and Scollari pulled up to the White Plains apartment of the woman who claimed to have seen the victims. Detective Burns had no confidence in this lead and believed that detectives from White Plains should be the ones questioning this caller. "I agree with Lieutenant Doore. The girls aren't from Lakeside. Why should we be here?"

"C'mon, Burns, are we only supposed to investigate crimes involving people from our town? If your daughter was found on the side of the road in another town, wouldn't you expect every cop in the area to be on it?" Scollari shut the engine and opened his door.

"Let's see what this girl has to say," he said with a bit more optimism than his partner had. "Hell, we may be able to solve this identity mystery and win appreciation for our department."

The young woman who answered the door was not an attention-seeker. She seemed to have actually seen the girls and wanted to help.

Detective Scollari led the questioning after they were settled into the kitchen.

Sharon Becket was 23 years old. She worked in an office building not far from where she said she saw the two victims about 12:30PM during her lunch break.

"I think I saw the two girls at the Galleria Mall. They looked like the girls in the paper."

The Galleria Mall is made up of stores designed to attract

young shoppers, particularly young female shoppers. There is a food court in addition to the various shops. It was not unusual for patrons to come to this mall from the Bronx because of its close proximity to the bus depot and train station. Although described in advertisements as an "upscale mall," the prices were more reasonable than the prices in the stores at the more fashionable mall in White Plains.

Ms. Becket's news was both encouraging and distressing. Distressing because the Galleria is usually full of young girls; the possibility that this witness was able to pick out our two victims from sketches in the newspaper was remote at best. It seemed encouraging because the transportation options allowed that the girls, even if from the Bronx, could have easily been in the mall.

Scollari asked, "Why were you at the mall that day?"

"I work here in White Plains at the office building across the street. I often go to the food court for lunch or to browse in some of the shops. This particular day I was on a lunch break."

Scollari nodded. "Can you remember anything about the girls, such as how old they looked, how tall, anything distinctive?"

The early news reports did not go into any specific details about the girls such as what they were wearing or their heights, relative to each other.

"They looked like teenagers, but I'm not really a good judge of age." Becket sipped some coffee. "They both looked similar in build and height. They weren't especially thin or fat; they looked like most of the girls I see there."

"Do you remember how they were dressed?" Scollari pressed.

"I do. I recall that they were both wearing really short skirts. I found that odd because of how cold it was."

Scollari made a note on his pad. "Did you see them go into any particular store?"

"No. I only saw them in the food court. I don't know where

they went from there. I got a coffee and went back to work."

Since Sharon Becket's description didn't match that of the two victims, Detective Scollari, reluctantly, decided to show her the copies of the morgue photos.

Sharon paled when she saw the images, Scollari thought she might pass out.

"Oh my God," she said weakly.

"I'm sorry to have to show you these. Your description didn't closely match our victims; this was the only way to be sure the victims were or were not the girls you saw at the mall."

"They look different in the pictures from the sketches I saw in the paper."

Detective Scollari looked at Detective Burns with resignation and with a nod of acknowledgement: Burns had been right in his lack of optimism. He then turned back to Sharon. "When was it that you think you saw them?"

"It was about four days ago."

It was obvious that Sharon had not seen the two victims. "I'm sorry for upsetting you with these pictures. Thank you very much for your help."

"Do you think they were the girls I saw?"

"More than likely, no, they weren't."

CHAPTER 18

Lieutenant Capanno and I made the short trip on Wednesday to Greenwich, Connecticut, in the hopes that this lead would help to identify our two victims. Detective Scollari had advised Lieutenant Capanno on Monday that the White Plains lead did not pan out.

The witness sighting was only a few days ago. Nowhere near our time of death for the girls.

Greenwich was a short drive on the Connecticut Merritt Parkway, which becomes the Hutchinson River Parkway in New York. Since the bodies were found close to the Hutch, the possibility that they were from Connecticut was feasible. The person we were on our way to meet was waiting for us in a diner close to the parkway.

When we entered the diner, we saw a gentleman in his early forties waving from one of the booths.

"Are you Mister Compton?" Lt. Capanno asked.

"Yes, I am."

"How did you know who we were? Is it that obvious that we're police officers?" the lieutenant smiled.

"I saw the unmarked car with New York plates pull up, I figured it out."

The man was obviously observant. He was stocky, with grey hair, dressed in casual attire. The jacket hanging on the rack next to his booth had some sort of patch on the sleeve, but I couldn't make out what it said.

Lieutenant Capanno and I sat across from Mr. Compton. "What do you do for a living, Sir?" Capanno asked.

"I'm a city bus driver. I usually work the afternoon shift."

"You have a good eye for detail." The lieutenant was looking for someone to take an order. "I need a cup of coffee," he said before continuing his questioning.

"Do you live here in Connecticut?" I decided to keep things moving.

"Yes, I live in Stamford."

"How did you see the story and pictures in the paper? So far, the story has been limited to the local newspaper in New York."

"My route takes me close to the New York border and I get a lot of New York riders on my bus. Sometimes they leave a paper behind. Yesterday I happened to pick one up; I saw the article and pictures."

The waitress came to take our orders. "Can I get anything for you, young man?"

"No, thank you ma'am. I'm good, but my friend here would like some coffee," I answered, and returned my attention to Compton.

With his coffee order in, the lieutenant got back to the interview. "Were the girls in the paper passengers on your bus?" The lieutenant was hoping he would say *yes* since that might give other important location clues, such as where they got on and off the bus.

"No, I didn't see them on the bus. I saw them here in this diner. That's why I asked you to meet me here."

"Was this the first time you saw these girls?" The coffee arrived and the lieutenant took a sip right away.

"Yes. I'm in this dinner often. Ever since my wife passed away, the people who work here have come to be like family."

"I'm sorry to hear about your wife. Do you have any family close by?"

"No, I have a brother who lives in Seattle. I see him every now and then when he comes east to visit his wife's family. They live in Massachusetts, so he tries to fit me in to his visits with them."

While Capanno took another sip of his coffee I asked, "When was it that you saw these two young ladies?"

"It was about three weeks ago."

"What time of day was it?"

"It was right before I was going to leave for work; I would say about 3:00 in the afternoon."

"How close a look did you get of them?"

"They sat at the counter and I was in my favorite booth here, which as you can see, is relatively close to the counter."

"How would you describe the two girls?"

"They looked to be in their late teens. Both were wearing long coats which they didn't take off, so I couldn't tell what they were wearing under the coats or guess at their build. But they didn't look heavy."

The time frame the medical examiner gave would allow this potential sighting to be a possibility. The clothing descriptions were not close, but it was possible that Compton saw them on a different day, not wearing the same clothing that they were found in.

Capanno let me continue with the questioning. "I'm going to show you some rather disturbing photos of the victims taken at the time of their autopsies. I'll understand if you have a reluctance to look at them."

"I'm trying to help and I understand how important it is for your investigation. Driving for a living, I've seen some pretty horrific traffic accidents. I'm sure pictures won't bother me."

Mr. Compton remained calm, his expression unchanged, as he carefully studied the morgue photos of the two girls. "I don't think these photos look much like the two girls I saw that day. The sketches in the paper had a slight resemblance, but these pictures look as if your victims may have been Hispanic. The two girls I saw didn't appear to be."

Mr. Compton looked up toward the cash register and said, "Crap, there's one of the girls I saw that day."

"Are you sure?" My voice remained steady, despite the let-down.

Yes, I'm positive. She's even wearing the same coat I saw that day."

Our optimism had quickly changed to disappointment. "We're happy that the girls you saw are still alive. We very much appreciate your help," Capanno said. "Coffee is great, I think I'll get one to go."

We went to the register, ordered coffee for ourselves, and Capanno picked up the check to pay for Mr. Compton's breakfast.

"You don't have to do that," he said from the booth.

Taking money out of his pocket, Capanno answered, "You were more help than you think. Eliminating possibilities is as important as proving them."

CHAPTER 19

Lieutenant Capanno decided to put the article and the sketches that had appeared in the morning papers into *El Tarino*, a newspaper available throughout Latino communities. Since the medical examiner felt at least one of the victims was of Hispanic origin, maybe a wider readership would yield a lead.

While checking on the distribution of the flyers, I got a phone call from a woman living in the Bronx. "Hello, I'm Officer DeMarco. How can I help you?"

"I know those girls you got in the newspaper, and I know who killed them."

I didn't want to sound over-anxious. "Can you give me your name?"

"Come down here, then I'll give you some information."

"Where is *here*?" No name was offered.

"You know Southern Boulevard? It's under the El" The El is the elevated subway train in the Bronx.

"I'm familiar with it," I said.

"How long does it take you to get down here?"

"Considering the traffic," I said, "probably about an hour."

"How will I recognize you?"

"I'll find you," she said, and hung up.

When I told Capanno, he said, "You and Scollari take this."

Detective Scollari was at his desk writing the report on the meeting he and Burns had shared with Ms. Becket.

Capanno interrupted Andy Scollari's typing. "Burns, you do the report. Andy and the kid have a lead that has to be followed."

Andy stopped typing mid-sentence, ready to join me.

As we were going out to the parking lot, I said, "You should have seen Burns' face when the lieutenant told him to write the report."

Andy chuckled, "I know Capanno wants it right away, so Burns won't be able to wrangle out of writing it."

It took us the full hour to reach our destination. We pulled our unmarked car to the front of Manny's Bodega. The place looked like a local dive, ripe for drug deals and other illegal activities, despite its efforts to look legit. A young Hispanic woman came outside and walked right up to our car.

"You must be the detectives. Let's go inside, it's cold out here."

Andy leaned toward her and asked, "How'd you know we weren't city cops, here to check on the neighborhood?"

"Ain't no cops down here dumb enough to drive around with hubcaps on their wheels and expect them to stay on the car very long."

She turned to go back to the bodega. We locked the car and followed her inside.

The bodega was small, with a couple of tables and chairs filling the space in the rear. The front consisted of crowded shelves and the register. A young guy sat behind the counter appearing to be reading a paper, never lifting his eyes from the print. I suppose if you don't look up, you can't bear witness to anything that goes on.

Once at the back of the store, which proved to be as dirty as it was small, Detective Scollari began the questioning. "It's time to tell us your name."

"Tania."

"Tania what?"

"Tania is all I'm gonna give you, all you need. How much you going to pay me for this information?" Tania answered flatly.

"If you provide information that leads to an arrest and

conviction, I'm sure there will be some sort of reward. But we're not able to give you anything at this time," Scollari answered in an equally emotionless tone.

It was starting to look as if Tania was trying to run a scam.

I took out my notebook and said, "Let's see if we can identify our victims and take it from there."

"OK, but I ain't givin you nuthin on the killins' without some reward."

I repeated, "Let's start with who the girls are."

"Them two was hookers right here on Southern Boulevard."

"Do you know their names?"

"I only knew them by their street names, Cleo and Short-stuff."

"Do... you... know... where... they... lived?" Andy asked slowly.

She realized we were getting annoyed. "I don't know where they were from, but I figure it was someplace close by because I never seen them in cars, taxis, or on the El"

"Did they usually work together?"

"I seen them together all the time. Sometimes they'd even leave with a John together."

Andy continued, "When was the last time you saw them?"

"About a week ago. I seen them get in some car with Jersey plates. I think it was a green Chevy."

We knew the victims had been on the side of the road longer than that; we pressed Tania to think about her recollection of the time more clearly. "Are you sure about the date?"

"Yeah, you could check it out because the two of them got busted by city cops."

"Which precinct?" I continued.

"The four-two."

"We'll check out the information you gave us with the four-two and see if they're our two victims."

"If your information turns out to be useful how do we get in touch with you?" Andy asked.

"Give me your card. I'll call you next week."

Andy gave Tania his card. "Why don't you call the detective division at Lakeside Police Department in about two hours; we should know by then if we need to talk further."

Detective Scollari and I drove directly to the forty-second Precinct. Inside the old building, we identified ourselves and asked the desk sergeant who we should speak with regarding the information Tania gave us.

Desk Sergeant Lynch, a large man who looked to be about fifty years old, barely looked up from his paperwork.

"We're working on a double homicide and are trying to identify our victims," I stated. "There was evidence that connected them or their killers to the Bronx,"

"Go upstairs and see Detective Johnson," he said without any change in his demeanor.

"Thanks, Sarge. Do you know if your precinct got any of our flyers on the case yet?"

Sergeant Lynch finally looked at us, "Not to my knowledge; if we did, one would be posted on our bulletin board. I don't think I saw anything from a Westchester PD."

I gave the sergeant two of the flyers and we went upstairs to find Detective Johnson. The four-two detective squad room was cluttered with desks that looked as if they had been there since the early 1900's, when the building was constructed. There were old manual typewriters on some of the desks and a caged area in the corner that looked more like a pen from the ASPCA than a holding cell for prisoners. We approached a detective who was pounding away on one of the antique typewriters.

Andy showed his detective shield. "We're from the Lakeside Police Department in Westchester. Can you tell us how to find Detective Johnson?"

Without missing a stroke of a key, he turned his head and using the cigar hanging from his mouth as a pointer, indicated the corner of the room and said, "There."

We followed the direction of the cigar. "There" at a desk in the corner of the room, sat Detective Johnson. He had clearly been around for a while.

"Grab a couple of chairs and sit down," he said, showing some interest.

I handed over a flyer and we explained why we were there, relating the information given to us by Tania.

Johnson smiled, "She's a piece of work, isn't she? Always looking to be paid for whatever bullshit she thinks we want to hear. She never gave us any information worth a dime. But she keeps trying."

"She told us she thinks our two victims are hookers named Cleo and Short-stuff.

"I'm familiar with the two hookers. They're not the victims. In fact," he continued, "I've been informed they're currently working in the Fiftieth Precinct on Eastchester Road, same precinct that houses the Emergency Services Unit."

"Tania told us she knew who killed the girls."

"She does that, hoping that we'll pay her something up front. How long have your victims been dead?"

"At least three to four weeks."

"Then they definitely can't be Cleo and Short-stuff. They've been busted in the Fiftieth more recently than that. Besides, they don't look anything like the girls on your flyers."

Andy called Lieutenant Capanno to tell him that we had hit another dead-end.

CHAPTER 20

L ieutenant Capanno decided to call in a psychic.
I was skeptical. From what I had read, officers receiving information from psychic *visions*, often made the mistake of associating anything similar to what the psychic said to the facts. This technique is called *retrofitting*, connecting the visions with known information. For example, the psychic may say, "I sense that *water* is important. A detective may then make an association to *River* Street, when River Street is not pertinent to the case, even though it is in the vicinity of the crime scene. The time spent following this type of lead uses valuable time and manpower. As I said, I was skeptical.

The psychic Capanno contacted was a volunteer who allegedly had helped other police departments throughout the country. Some of the detectives working the case perceived this as an act of desperation by the lieutenant. They saw it as an indication that he didn't trust their investigative skills. I was not going to question his approach; I respected him as a good investigator not easily swayed by unproven methods and a lieutenant who appreciated his detectives. However, like most of the members of the detective division, I remained doubtful of the validity of claims made by psychics.

The first time I met Wanda was at police headquarters; she had already met with the lieutenant twice before. The lieutenant seemed impressed with whatever she told him, even though it had not moved us any closer to identifying the victims or suspects.

Capanno and Wanda were in the interview room at

headquarters. Wanda was looking at and handling some of the personal effects of our two victims. When he saw me arrive, Lieutenant Capanno stepped out into the hallway and invited me in to meet the psychic and listen to see if anything she said might be helpful.

"Do you really think she can give us anything useful?" I had to ask.

"Well, she told me some things that make me curious about her abilities."

"You know that I don't really give much credence to this, but if you think it will help, I'll listen."

I followed Capanno into the room. My skepticism only increased as I watched Wanda "perform." Wanda was a large woman, wearing a colorful shawl and a large brimmed hat. Around her neck were several strands of beads, some of which had feathers on them.

"I see Hispanic names, *Juan*, *Hector* and *Juanita*," she said as she held her fingers against her temples. I assumed that was an indication of her visions.

"We suspect at least one of our victims is Hispanic. Perhaps your vision could include a last name or telephone number," I prompted.

She quickly sized me up as a nonbeliever.

Wanda picked up one of the keys, closed her eyes— and held it to her forehead. "I see a red door."

"Does the door happen to have a number on it?" She opened her eyes and looked at me with unmasked aversion.

"I don't see anything else at this time. I must empty my head of negative thoughts." I laughed to myself at her direct aim at me.

I left the room shaking my head. "If she's truly psychic," I thought, "she knows exactly what I think of her." I did not see Wanda again.

None of the other officers assigned to the investigation met with her, nor heard her alleged contributions to the case. The lieutenant, however, met with her several more times, ironically to me, always at a restaurant where the meeting included a free meal. The lieutenant was content to keep her value — or lack thereof — to himself.

The best piece of hard evidence we had was the key that connected the crime to the Bronx. No piece of evidence is too small.

Resolving to pursue this connection, I went to my desk and pulled out my notes and reports to make sure nothing had been missed and to ensure all possible NYPD precincts had received the flyers.

CHAPTER 21

Friday, April 6th

Maria Ramos walked into the housing police precinct, New York City Police Service Area 8 headquarters early Friday morning at about 11AM.

Maria had made the trip to PSA 8 almost daily for two months since reporting her daughter missing on February 5th, to learn if any progress had been made in a search her daughter, Crystal. She approached the desk area and was greeted again by Sergeant O'Hara, a longtime veteran of the police department.

"Hello Maria. ¿Cómo estás hoy?"

"Hello Sergeant. Estoy bien. How are you?"

In a tearful voice, Mrs. Ramos said, "I want to know if you have any information about my Crystal."

Sergeant O'Hara motioned Mrs. Ramos to a seat in one of the chairs by the bulletin board in the lobby. "Can I get you a cup of coffee? I'm sorry there is no news." He felt sorry for the woman, who came in so often, desperately looking for help in finding her daughter.

"No, gracias," Maria answered, dejected.

As she was getting up to leave, Maria Ramos saw the Lakeside Police Department flyer on the bulletin board. She instantly recognized one of the photos as her daughter. She choked, "Dios mía!, es mi hija."

Sergeant O'Hara heard her sob and ran from behind the desk to grab her in case she fainted.

"What is it, Maria?" O'Hara asked.

Pointing at the flyer, Mrs. Ramos almost screamed, "That is my Crystal, Es mi hija!"

"Are you sure, Maria?"

"Sí! Yes, that is her. Oh, Dios. You found her?"

"Hold on a moment, Maria." He motioned to another officer. "Bring her up to Canazzaro," O'Hara put his hand on Ramos' shoulder. "This officer will help you upstairs."

O'Hara picked up the phone and dialed. "Canazzaro, Peterson is bringing a Mrs. Ramos up to see you. She says her daughter is the victim on one of the flyers from Westchester PD."

Canazzaro sucked down some coffee. "You sure, Sarge?"

"Christ! She practically passed out when she saw the flyer."

Canazzaro looked up to see Officer Peterson helping Maria to his desk. "Thanks, Sarge, she's here now."

Mrs. Ramos sat in the chair next to Detective Angel Canazzaro's desk. He offered her a box of tissues and asked, "Can I get you some water?"

"No, gracias. Where is the picture of my Crystal from?"

Canazzaro turned to Peterson. "Go downstairs and bring me the flyers from Lakeside."

While he was waiting for Peterson to return, he said, "Are you *sure*, ma'am?"

Maria opened her purse. "Sí. I have pictures."

Peterson returned with the flyers. Canazzaro looked at the pictures Mrs. Ramos gave him and compared details to the information on the flyer. He immediately noticed that in one of the photos of Crystal, she was wearing a sweater-jacket that matched the description of the jacket on the Lakeside Police flyer.

Canazzaro pointed at the photo. "She was wearing that sweater when she left the house?"

"Sí, I told her it was too cold for such a sweater."

Mrs. Ramos began to cry as she recalled arguing with her

daughter about the sweater and insisting that it wasn't warm enough for the cold weather. She stared at the flyer with the painful awareness that the young woman on the flyer was no longer alive.

Canazzaro knew that the only way to say it was to say it. "Yes, Mrs. Ramos. I am sorry. She is dead." Canazzaro handed Mrs. Ramos a cup of water from the cooler. "Drink some water, Mrs. Ramos."

Mrs. Ramos faced the cold realization that her fifteen-year-old daughter was gone.

Canazzaro held the other flyer Peterson gave him. "Can I show you another picture?"

"You have another picture of Crystal?" she asked.

"No ma'am," he said, showing her the picture of Lola, which she obviously missed, "this is a girl found with Crystal."

"You found someone else with my Crystal?"

Detective Canazzaro handed the other flyer to her.

Ramos buried her face in hands, "Dios mío. That is Lola. Crystal was with Lola the last day I saw her."

"Do you know Lola's last name?" Canazzaro asked gently, while getting as much information as he could.

"I am sorry, no. I only know her by *Lola*." Mrs. Ramos took a couple of additional pictures out of her purse. "This is Lola with Crystal."

"Do you know where Lola lived?"

"On Simpson Street, but I don't know the number. Lola was older than Crystal. She and my bambina were very close. Lola was supposed to be going into the Army soon. I think her brother and father were in jail for some bad things. That's all I know." She paused then asked, "You think someone in her family did this thing?"

"We don't have any other information. The Lakeside police are in charge of the investigation. That's where the girls were found, Mrs. Ramos."

"¿Dónde es Lakeside?" she asked.

"Westchester County."

She seemed confused, "That is upstate, no?"

"It's not that far away, Mrs. Ramos. I'll take you home now. I'll come to your home with the Lakeside police if that's OK."

"Sí, that is good," she sighed heavily, "You will come back to my house today?"

Canazzaro picked up the phone and dialed the Lakeside PD. "Yes, as soon as the other police department's officer gets here. Let me take you home. Is anyone else there?"

"No, mi marido está en el trabajajo."

Canazzaro asked her to call her husband at his job and have him meet her at their home. He handed her the receiver and offered to dial the number. "Would you like me to speak with him first?"

Mrs. Ramos shook her head, *no*, and took the phone from the detective. The conversation was held between sobs, but it was clear that Mr. Ramos would be home by the time his wife arrived.

Canazzaro drove Mrs. Ramos home and walked her to her apartment door. "I'll be back as soon as the Lakeside officer gets here." He waited until she opened the door and fell into the arms of her husband before he turned to leave.

"Don't take your coat off, Rocco," Lieutenant Capanno said, "you're going to the Bronx. We just got a call from a Detective Angel Canazzaro from the housing police. He said he has a woman who identified one of our girls as her daughter." I had just walked in from grabbing a fast lunch at the deli.

"PSA 8 is on Randall Avenue in the Bronx. Don't ask me where the hell that is. You'll find it."

"I'm sure I will, Lieu."

"Rocco, I don't suppose you're fluent in Spanish?"

"Sorry Lieu," I shrugged and headed out to the Bronx. I

was grateful that traffic was light and surprised with the ease of finding PSA 8. I entered the PSA building and approached the desk. Sergeant O'Hara looked up, "You must be the detective from Westchester."

"DeMarco, Lakeside PD."

O'Hara motioned toward the stairs. "Detective Canazzaro is waiting for you."

Angel Canazzaro was thirty-eight years old, a large man with a neatly trimmed beard. He was a seasoned detective with more than his share of challenging cases under his belt. We shook hands. "Canazzaro. Nice to meet you, Detective...?"

"DeMarco, Officer DeMarco."

"*Officer* DeMarco?" He repeated. He was expecting a detective.

"Yeah, it's a long story. I understand from my lieutenant we're going to the home of the mother of one of the girls."

Grabbing his coat and keys, he said, "Yes, an apartment complex on Union and 161st Street."

"Detective, OK for me to leave my car out front?"

He chuckled. "Not if you want it to be there when we get back. You can put it in the lot with our units."

"Please, call me Angel," he said as we pulled out of the police lot.

I looked at him and smiled, "Rocco," I said.

"Great," he laughed and added, tongue-in-cheek, "a couple of good Irish cops."

"My lieutenant called the M.E.'s office to see if we could bring Mrs. Ramos in to identify the bodies. We got the all-clear. Do you think she will be ready for that?"

"Yeah, I think she'll be OK. Her husband will be with her. I wanted you to meet Mrs. Ramos today, with me, so she knows who she'll be dealing with moving forward. I promised her I'd be back with you. After we explain the arrangements with the M.E., we can leave. I don't think it would be a good idea to pump her for too much information today."

I shook my head in agreement, "Sounds good."

We parked on 161st Street. Angel didn't seem to concerned about the safety of his car. He must have sensed I wasn't as confident, "Don't worry," he smiled. "If it's not here when we come out, we'll call for the police."

We both laughed and headed into the building, knowing that would be our last light moment for the day.

When we entered the Ramos apartment, Mrs. Ramos led us to some comfortable chairs and offered coffee. Angel refused politely for both of us.

"This is Officer DeMarco from the Lakeside Police Department."

I stood and gently shook Mrs. Ramos' hand. "I am sorry about your daughter." I motioned for her to sit down next to me. "Mrs. Ramos, I know this isn't going to be easy. We need you to come with us tomorrow to identify Crystal. Will you be alright with that?"

She nodded her head. "Sí, lo entiendo. It will be OK. My marido will be with me. He is Crystal's stepfather, but he loves her very much." Mr. Ramos had been standing quietly in the doorway to the kitchen. He nodded.

She was still referring to her daughter in the present tense.

"Can you ask Mrs. Ramos, in Spanish, to remember anything to help confirm the identification, things such as scars, operations or injuries Crystal had...anything that would help the M.E."

"She's pretty good with English," he said, but he went on to explain, in Spanish, what she could do to help. Angel said, "We will pick you and Mr. Ramos up tomorrow morning. He gave her his card and said, "Llámame si necesitas algo."

We closed the door behind us and left the devastated couple to cope with their tragedy.

CHAPTER 22

The next morning, I picked up Detective Canazzaro and we drove to the Ramos apartment to take Mr. and Mrs. Ramos to the Medical Examiner's office.

I waited in the car while Canazzaro went up to get Crystal's parents.

He returned in a few minutes with Francisco and Maria Ramos and helped them settle into the back of the car.

Mr. Ramos, not as fluent in English, as his wife, asked, "¿Qué es el médico forense?"

Angel suspected incorrectly that I hadn't understood what Mr. Ramos asked and explained to him, "Es el depósito de cadáveres."

Mrs. Ramos began to cry.

I turned to Angel, "I imagine there isn't a less upsetting way to say that, no matter what the language."

When we arrived at the Medical Examiner's office, Mr. Ramos remarked, "This did not take too long, ¿Es el norte?"

I faced the *upstate* confusion so many times that I understood the question – even in Spanish. "This isn't upstate, Mr. Ramos. We are just over the line from the Bronx. Places such as Albany and Buffalo are upstate. Have you heard of those places?"

Mr. Ramos had not understood.

Mrs. Ramos, putting her hand on her husband's leg said, "Yes, Crystal would tell me they get very much snow, more than us."

I introduced Detective Canazzaro and Mr. and Mrs. Ramos

to Dr. Lowman. Dr. Lowman asked calmly, "Can I get you anything, coffee, water?"

"No, gracias, Doctor." Maria said. Mr. Ramos looked at his wife then said to Dr. Lowman, "Gracias, no, Doctor."

"You won't be in the same room as your daughter," Dr. Lowman said quietly to the Ramos'. He directed us into a small room with a large window covered by a maroon curtain hung from the opposite side. Dr. Lowman explained that the young woman's body would be wheeled into the room on the other side of the curtain and, when the Mr. and Mrs. Ramos were ready, the curtain would be opened for the viewing.

"You let us know when you are ready for us to open the curtain," he said.

Dr. Lowman was notified when the body was brought into the room. He asked Mr. and Mrs. Ramos if they were ready.

Mr. Ramos whispered, "Sí."

Mrs. Ramos was shaking her head *no* as she was saying, "Sí." Lowman understood: she was ready, but did not want to see her baby's dead body.

When the curtain opened, we saw the body on a gurney covered by a sheet. Only Crystal's head was exposed. I was relieved that the autopsy cuts were not visible and I was amazed that her head showed no signs of the procedure Dr. Lowman performed on the young woman's brain.

Mrs. Ramos began to cry. Afraid she would faint, I moved to stand behind her.

"Dios mío." Mr. Ramos, who hadn't shown much emotion to this point, also became visibly shaken by the sight of his step-daughter.

The parents confirmed the identity of their daughter, Crystal Ramos. Mrs. Ramos spoke briefly with Dr. Lowman about the scars and injuries she had been asked to remember.

Later, we helped Mr. and Mrs. Ramos make arrangements to have Crystal's body picked up by a Bronx funeral home. Wordlessly, we drove the parents back to their home.

After dropping Mr. and Mrs. Ramos off at their home, I took Angel back to his headquarters. Before getting out of the car, he looked at me and offered more help. "I'll try to make contact with any Army recruiters in the area of Simpson Street in hopes Lola used one of them. You and I will stay in touch."

"Angel, thanks for your help."

I headed back to headquarters.

CHAPTER 23

Sunday, April 8th

Lieutenant Capanno was in the office when I arrived. Our work was demanding a 7-day schedule. He told me that Smitty was still out sick and that I would have to continue on my own. I was fine with that.

I told the lieutenant that Mrs. Ramos was expecting me. "She has more pictures of the girls, Lieu, I want to take a look at them."

"Any problem communicating, Rocco? Is her English OK?"

"No problem." I grabbed the keys to one of the older unmarked vehicles. "I'll take the hubcaps off before I leave." I shot a smile back at the lieutenant.

I went back to the apartment building that Crystal had lived in on 161st Street near Union Avenue. I hadn't really paid attention to the condition of the building the previous day. The building was an eighteen-story high-rise with ten to twelve apartments on each floor. Mrs. Ramos lived on the twelfth floor.

The walls of the elevator were covered with graffiti, *gang tags*, which identified particular gangs and marked their turf. The bare bulb in the elevator ceiling gave only a shadow of light. I got off on the twelfth floor and approached apartment 1207. Mrs. Ramos answered my knock. It was obvious from her red, puffy eyes she had not had much sleep.

"Buenos días, officer." She sounded apologetic, "Mi marido

está en el trabajo. In English she said, "Sorry, my husband is at work; I will help you today."

Mrs. Ramos led me into the clean kitchen, which held a warm, strong aroma of coffee.

"¿Quiere café?" she asked as if she had read my mind.

"Yes, please."

I took a sip of the hot coffee.

Mrs. Ramos smiled, sensing I didn't drink Spanish coffee very often. "Is too strong for you?"

"No," I said politely. "It's fine. It will keep me awake today!"

That put a smile on her face and helped ease the tension of the morning. Little did I know then, that cup of coffee would keep me awake for three days.

It was time to get to Crystal's disappearance and death. Mrs. Ramos handed me a stack of about fifty photos. "These are some pictures my Crystal took. She was always taking pictures."

I thumbed through the pictures and asked, "Do you know many of the people in these pictures?"

Maria started to tear up. "Is this too hard for you, Señora Ramos?"

She wiped her eyes, "No, I will be OK. I want to help. I do not know many of Crystal's friends in these pictures. Some only have *apados*, what you call *nicknames*. Some, I know first names only."

There were many photos of Lola and some with Lola and Crystal. The same young man appeared in several photos.

"Mrs. Ramos," I asked, pointing to the man in one of the photos, "Do you know who this is?"

Maria studied the picture then looked at others in which he appeared. "His name is Danny. I don't know him well, only from Crystal talking about him."

"Do you know his last name?"

"Lo siento," she said apologetically. "Crystal says he and his father have a club near here. Trinity Avenue, I think."

"Did Crystal go to this club?"

Shaking her head, she said, "I hope no. It is not for young people."

I picked up the stack of pictures. "Can I keep these? I will give them back to you after the investigation."

"Sí. I hope they help you find this *monstruo* that took my Crystal."

"When is Crystal's funeral?"

"El servicio funerario es Miércoles....a las nueve por la mañana, at la iglesia de Saint Teresa, cerca de 152nd Street." Tears welled up in her eyes again.

Even with my limited understanding of Spanish, I understood where and when. I put my jacket on. "Gracias, Señora. I will stay in touch with you. If you need me, here is the phone number to our detective division." She took the card. "I also wrote Detective Canazzaro's name and number on the back. If you can think of anything that would help us identify Lola, please call."

I took her hand. "I will work hard to try to find out who did this to Crystal, Mrs. Ramos."

"I know you will detective. Vaya con dios."

I would attend Crystal's funeral to see who showed up and to try to discover the names of some of the people in the photographs that Mrs. Ramos gave me.

CHAPTER 24

When I got back to Lakeside headquarters, I was greeted by Sergeant Edwards. "Well, if it isn't the leader of our Bronx task force," he said with a smile. "We're all starting to wonder how long it will take you to transfer down there."

I couldn't help but laugh. "Not a chance, Sarge. The deli's in the Bronx don't compare to ours. And I sure would miss your smile every morning."

"You just missed a call from a Detective Canazzaro from PSA8. He wants you to call him back, says it's important. Sounds like you're making some progress down there."

"I think we are."

Edwards nodded and handed me the phone message. "Here's his info. He says it has something to do with the identity of the second girl."

"Thanks, Sarge, I'll call him right now."

When I dialed the Bronx office, Detective Anderson answered the call.

"Hello, Detective. This is Officer DeMarco from the Lakeside PD, returning Detective Canazzaro's call."

"The detective has today off. Can I take a message?"

I tried to convey the urgency of my call.

Anderson understood. "OK, give me your number. I'll call Angel at home and have him call back you ASAP."

Detective Canazzaro got back to me within minutes. "Rocco, I have more information. A contact at the local Army recruiting office told me Lola was scheduled to leave for basic training in February."

"I assume he was able to give you a last name and address."

"You assume right, my friend. The full name is Lola Vasquez. She lived at 1645 Simpson Street. I'll go with you if you want."

"I'm sure my Lieutenant will want to go with me. Enjoy the rest of your day off, Angel. I'll stay in touch."

"Take down my home phone number in case you need me. Good luck, Rocco."

I called the lieutenant at home to share the new information.

"Wait at HQ. You, me and Scollari will go together. I have no idea how long Smitty is going to be out, so I want someone else onboard each step of the way. I'll give Andy a call and we'll meet you in fifteen minutes.

Andy Scollari arrived at headquarters before the lieutenant. "What's up Rocco? Did you go to Mrs. Ramos' house?"

"I went there this morning." I smiled, "If you want to stay wide awake, accept her offer of coffee."

"Was she able to give you any more information about Lola?"

"No, but I did get a call from Angel Canazzaro. He found the recruiter who provided him with Lola's full address. Lieutenant Capanno is joining us to drive over as soon as he gets here. We'll speak with anyone who's living there."

Capanno was lighting a cigarette as he entered headquarters. "Give me a minute to check in with the squad at the 41st before we leave. I'll give them a heads-up that we'll be in the area."

Capanno drove and, thankfully, didn't light up inside the car. I grew to hate the smell of cigarette smoke after I quit, now almost three years ago.

Simpson Street was in a run-down neighborhood in what was probably one of the worst sections of the Bronx. On the narrow street were stripped cars and shoddy tenements with bags of uncollected garbage piled in front.

Capanno visually scoured the block. "Rocco, what address are we looking for?"

"1645 Simpson, Lieu." I had been looking at the buildings for those with numbers and saw an empty parking spot in the 1600-range. "If we park here, we should be pretty close."

Capanno, kept scanning the street. "I wonder if one of us should stay with the car." He was only half-joking.

As we approached the entrance to 1645, Capanno blurted, "Look! The door is red! Just like Wanda pictured."

I didn't want to spoil my boss' moment, so I refrained from pointing out that most of the doors were painted a dingy red.

There is no other way to describe it: the lobby was disgusting. The old paint on the walls, where not covered by graffiti, was peeling. Tiles that may have been part of a decorative feature when the building was new were chipped or missing. Floor tiles were missing as well, exposing filthy cement. The lobby had the stench of stale urine. None of us spoke.

The apartment we were looking for was on the third floor of this ten-story building, apartment 3A. The smell on the third floor was no better than the lobby.

The woman who answered our knock was as dilapidated as the building itself. Both she and her clothing appeared neglected, "Who are you people?" she asked as she exhaled a gray cloud of smoke from the stub of the cigarette she was smoking.

Capanno introduced us. "We're from the Lakeside Police Department ma'am. Are you Mrs. Vasquez?"

In a gravelly voice, perhaps the result of years of smoking, she said, "Yeah, that's me. I'm Eva Vasquez. What do you want?"

Capanno remained professional. "I'm afraid we have some sad news for you about your daughter, Lola."

Seemingly unmoved, Mrs. Vasquez said, "Sad news? Where the hell is Lakeside?"

Without waiting for answers, she continued, "What did she do? Get herself arrested in some upstate town? Great, now she'll lose her job."

The lieutenant ignored the reference to *upstate*. He looked directly at Mrs. Vasquez, "She wasn't arrested, Mrs. Vasquez. She's been murdered." He took the flyer with the picture of Lola taken at the morgue from his jacket pocket. "Please take a look at this. Is it your daughter?"

For a moment, Mrs. Vasquez saddened and nodded. "Where was she killed?"

"We don't know where she was murdered. She and another girl were found in our town, Lakeside."

Mrs. Vasquez lost any sadness she may have felt a moment ago. "Who was this other girl? she asked without emotion.

Capanno showed her Crystal's picture. "Crystal Ramos."

"Oh, that little bitch?" Mrs. Vasquez scoffed. "What do you want from me?"

Capanno did not react to Eva's reference to Crystal. He maintained his even tone, "You will have to go the Westchester Medical Examiner's office to make a positive identification. Do you have any other family members who can accompany you?"

"No. My worthless husband and son are in prison for robbery. So now I have no one to help me make ends meet. Damn Lola."

Andy and I threw a look at each other. Her daughter was no more than a meal ticket.

"Do you work?" the lieutenant remained neutral and professional, while Andy and I were starting to show our contempt.

Eva Vasquez put a fresh cigarette in her mouth. "Got a light?" Then she answered, "No, I'm on public assistance."

The lieutenant said, "We will have the police take you to the morgue to make the identification."

"Do I have to go to see the body?" she sighed. "I can tell by the picture you showed me that it's Lola."

Lieutenant Capanno said, "A personal identification is needed. You will have to go." He pushed ahead, "Mrs. Vasquez, can I show you some pictures? Maybe you can try to identify anyone who might help us with our investigation?"

She let out another sigh and said, "Sure. I guess so. Here, sit at the table."

She and the lieutenant sat at a small table in the space near the living room. There were empty vodka bottles and an ashtray overflowing with cigarette butts taking up most of the tabletop.

Capanno lit yet another cigarette for her. "You will have to make arrangements with a funeral parlor to pick up Lola's body."

Vasquez exhaled some smoke. "I don't have money for putting her in a funeral home and I don't have relatives who need to see her."

"Are you and Lola Catholic?"

She shrugged. "Yeah, I guess. Lola went to St. Teresa's sometimes. I guess I could probably get a mass there. Do you think social services will help with the burial and pay for a funeral home to pick her up?"

The lieutenant was beginning to lose patience. "I imagine you could get some help from them, but I don't know how much."

I took a seat on a chair near the table and Andy sat nearby on a cushioned chair in the living room. When I turned to share a look with Andy, a look that would acknowledge all the distaste I knew we were both feeling toward Vasquez and the filth surrounding her, I saw him step on and squash a large cockroach that was scurrying away from the commotion in the room — back to its nest nearby. That said it all. I turned my attention back to the lieutenant and Mrs. Vasquez.

Capanno handed some of the photos from Crystal's mother to Mrs. Vasquez. "I don't know any of these people," she said, "maybe this little fat guy." Mrs. Vasquez looked at the pictures more closely through a cloud of smoke. "His name is Danny."

She sat up straight as if she had given us the singular solution to our case. "I seen him at the club he and his father have."

"Where is this club?" Capanno asked.

When Eva Vasquez shrugged as if trying to remember, I leaned over to the lieutenant and said, "I'll fill you in on that Lieu, with the information I got from Mrs. Ramos."

"Mrs. Vasquez, Detective Scollari will pick you up tomorrow and take you to the M.E.'s office for identification and to make arrangements to have Lola's body picked up." Mrs. Vasquez looked in Andy's direction, fortunately he was no longer killing bugs; he nodded, acknowledging the arrangement.

As we rose to leave, Capanno gave Mrs. Vasquez his business card. "Please call us if you think of anything that will help identify Lola's killer or killers."

"Yeah. Like that's gonna get me back the paycheck she was bringin' home."

CHAPTER 25

Tuesday, April 10th

The Lieutenant told me to take Monday off since I had not had much time off since the case started. I was back at work first thing Tuesday morning.

Detective Smith was still out sick, so I remained partnered with Andy Scollari. We drove to St. Teresa's Church in the Bronx for Lola's funeral. It was the same church at which Crystal's funeral would be held the following day.

Our intention was to see who would come to the funeral and to identify any who resembled the faces in the photographs Mrs. Ramos gave us.

As we looked through the small group of ten to twelve people, I spotted Mrs. Vasquez. "I'll be damned," I said to Andy. "Lola's heartless mother showed up and looks respectful in her black dress. You think she got it special for the funeral?"

Andy shook his head. "No. I think it's something she had. She was not going to spend any money; after all, her source of income is in that coffin." Then he turned to me, "But I agree with you Rocco, I'm surprised she showed up looking presentable."

"Anyone in that group look like someone in our pictures?" I asked him.

Andy took a look at some of the pictures and then at the people. "Nope, nobody stands out."

We remained close to the rear door of the church during

the service; in case anyone came in late, we would see his or her face. When the ceremony was over, we stayed there to get a closer, second look at the people as they were leaving.

I strained to get a better look at one young woman as she passed us. "How about her?" I motioned toward the woman with my head while holding up one of the pictures for Andy.

Andy looked at her and then at the picture again. "I think she does look like someone in that picture with both girls."

We casually approached the young woman. "Excuse me miss," Andy began, "can we ask you a couple of questions about Lola?" He took his badge out of his jacket pocket.

I showed her my identification as well. "I'm officer DeMarco and this is Detective Scollari. We're investigating Lola's death. What is your name?"

She examined Andy's badge closely. "Rhonda Rodriquez."

Rhonda seemed satisfied that we were cops. "What precinct you from?"

"We aren't NYPD," I said. "We're from Lakeside, New York."

"Where the hell is that?" she asked, looking at Andy's badge again.

It was time for me to explain, again, where Lakeside was to another denizen of the Bronx, "It's near White Plains."

"Oh, I've heard of White Plains."

We showed her one of the pictures. "That's me with Lola and Crystal. Where'd you get the pictures from?"

"Crystal's mother gave them to me." I showed her the small stack of pictures.

She shrugged her shoulders as she shuffled through the photographs. "I was friendlier with Lola because she was my age. I didn't hang out much with Crystal 'cause she was just a kid. I only saw her when she was with Lola. I don't know why Lola hung out with her, but, hey, it's not my business." She paused. "You know though, I'm surprised Crystal isn't here."

Andy looked directly at Rhonda to see her reaction and said, "Crystal is dead as well."

Rhonda seemed surprised. "Wow! Were they together?"

Nodding my head, I said, "Yes, they were found alongside the roadway in Lakeside."

With almost a chuckle she said, "That sucks for you. I'm sure you guys are not used to doing much in the Bronx."

"Well, we're here now," I said, "and we could use some help from you. When was the last time you saw Lola?"

"Hmm, must have been a couple of weeks ago, at a bodega near Simpson Street."

"Was Crystal with her?" Andy asked.

"I don't think so, but I can't be sure, 'cause they were usually together. Like I said, I never got that, considering the age difference."

"Could she have been with someone else? Like a guy?"

"I doubt that," she said with a smile. Crystal was just a kid."

The picture of Rhonda with Lola and Crystal had Danny in the background.

I asked her to take a closer look at the picture. "Do you know who the guy in this picture with you and the girls is? We think his first name is Danny."

She squinted her eyes as if to focus. "I'm not sure who he is. Maybe I seen him before but I don't know him."

As you said," I repeated with a touch of sarcasm, "We don't get to the Bronx that often. Do you know where this picture was taken?"

"Could have been anywhere. Crystal was always taking pictures." She looked down at the photograph. "Let me look at it again. I think this one was near P.S. 62 in Hunts Point." She smiled at us. "Watch yourself, that's a bad area." She wasn't wrong. Hunts point was a very bad section of the Bronx.

I smiled at Rhonda. "I think we'll manage to take care of ourselves. Do you hang out there often?"

"Not too much, like I said, it's a bad neighborhood. It's

easy to get to, though, as it's only a couple of blocks away from Southern Blvd."

"Where do you live, Rhonda?" I asked.

"I live with my grandmother on Union Avenue, near Jackson."

Considering how close to Crystal's house at 161st and Union was, I wondered if she knew Crystal better than she admitted. Andy gave her one of his business cards. "If you hear anything about the deaths of Lola and Crystal, give us a call."

I added, "We're coming back for Crystal's funeral tomorrow. Will you be here?"

"Yeah, I guess so."

As we turned to leave, Andy said, "If you think of anything that might help, let us know tomorrow."

We decided to check in with the detectives at the 41st Precinct to see if they could help with any of the people in the pictures or give us any further information about Rhonda Rodriguez. It was late afternoon when we arrived at the 41st to introduce ourselves and explain the crime we were investigating.

"I'm sorry," said a burly detective named Hanlon. "You guys gotta remember what NYPD is dealing with. What would be five years of crime for you, is what we deal with in a couple of days."

I nodded. "These kids have families." I handed him the photographs.

Hanlon nodded and flipped through the stack of pictures. "I don't recognize anybody right off." He handed them back to Andy. "Whatever help you need, feel free to ask; we're glad you're handling this one. I hope you nail whoever did this." That was our dismissal.

"Thanks," I said. We headed back to Lakeside in heavy, rush-hour traffic.

CHAPTER 26

As soon as the detectives left, Rhonda Rodriquez went to Danny's club. Danny was in the club alone, which made Rhonda less uneasy about being there. Like most of the nicer young women who knew of the club, she stayed away, avoiding the leering and propositioning from the men who hung out there. Prostitutes went to the club regularly; the men there were easy targets and would usually pay well for a quickie with a younger woman.

Rhonda, however, was not a hooker and the thought of one of these men touching her made her skin crawl. Danny and Rhonda had an easy, platonic friendship. She did not trust Danny's father, though, and was glad he wasn't there.

"Holá, Danny. Where's your father?

"He went to Atlantic City with some friends for a couple of days," Danny announced, and then added proudly, "I'm running the club while he's away."

Rhonda had to laugh at Danny's apparent belief that he had been left in charge of a high-end, important club. "Don't you usually keep the door locked when your dad's not here?"

"I can handle things," he said defensively. "I got it covered."

Rhonda thought to herself, "Yeah, if anything went down, you'd be the first one out the door."

"What're you doing here anyway, Rhonda? It's not like you to just drop in."

Rhonda got serious. "I was at Lola's funeral this morning. There were a couple of detectives from upstate showing pictures of Lola and Crystal and some of their friends. They asked me if I knew who any of the people in the pictures were. One of the pictures had you in it. But I didn't say I knew you. You'd better know that somebody is bound to identify you."

Rhonda noticed that Danny looked nervous. "Lola's dead?"

His question sounded fishy...not convincing as a question, but Rhonda bought his act. "Yeah, she was killed somewhere and dumped in some upstate town."

Danny began pacing. "Why am I in her stupid pictures?"

"Why are you pissed at being in some pictures, Danny?"

Danny's anxiety caused his voice to rise, "That little bitch was always taking pictures. Where is that little bitch Crystal? I want her to destroy all the pictures she has of me."

"Crystal is dead too, Danny. She and Lola were found together." Rhonda was surprised that Danny was so mad at Crystal for taking pictures. Danny usually wanted to be part of things and eagerly posed for pictures with the girls.

Danny rubbed his face. "I don't need this shit."

"Why are you so mad? You liked to be in pictures with the girls. What could those cops possibly ask about you? Do you know something?" Rhonda was starting to get suspicious.

Danny continued to pace around the room. "I don't need my father getting shit. He doesn't need a bunch of cops snooping around here. This is an illegal club."

"Wake up, Danny," Rhonda said, trying to get him to stop pacing and fidgeting. "I doubt that a couple of upstate cops are concerned about this little hole in the wall." Danny shot Rhonda a glare: he liked to think he was running the Bronx version of Caesar's Palace.

Danny stared directly at Rhonda. "What do you know about what they're looking for?"

Danny seemed far more nervous and afraid of the cops than annoyed about being in the pictures. "I don't know exactly what they want other than information that might help them figure out what happened to Lola and Crystal. They said they'd be at Crystal's funeral tomorrow. You going?"

Danny shook his head adamantly. "No way! I don't want them cops grilling me."

Rhonda was confused by Danny's behavior and thought it was odd, even for him. The dim-witted Danny was usually calm and easy-going; now he seemed terrified. "Look," she said, "I'll probably go. If you change your mind, let me know. I'm outta here now; I just wanted to let you know that the cops are asking about Crystal's pictures and you're in some of them."

As soon as Rhonda was gone, Danny decided to close the club until his dad got back. In case the upstate cops somehow found the club, the door would be locked and he would be nowhere in sight.

Danny drove over to Cubano's. He was relieved that Cubano was alone. As crazy as Cubano was, his behavior was always worse when Enrique and Bernardo were around. Also, Cubano did not seem to be high on coke, so Danny felt less afraid to give Cubano the news about the cops. Cubano was less erratic when he wasn't high.

"Holá, Danny. Why are you here? Need to buy something to make you high?' Maybe something to sell to your friends?" Cubano snickered.

"No, amigo." Danny said, happy that Cubano was in a good mood. "I just want to let you know about something that I just found out." Danny puffed up slightly, feeling important as the bearer of the news.

"Some upstate cops found Lola and Crystal." Danny cleared his throat and lowered his voice, "And they know who they were. The cops were at Lola's funeral today asking about pictures that Crystal took. They wanted to know about other people who were in the pictures."

Cubano's good mood suddenly changed. "What pictures? What fucking people?"

"Crystal's mother must have given the pictures to the cops. Crystal was always taking pictures."

Cubano got in Danny's face. "Did that little bitch have any pictures of me?"

Any self-importance and self-confidence Danny was feeling disappeared in an instant. He tried to back up, "No, the night they were here was the only time she ever saw you."

Cubano calmed down, "So what the fuck do I care about some upstate pigs asking questions about the two *putas*?" Then he was back in Danny's face, poking his forehead, "Remember, you and your old man know about what went down here. You two estan *altura sus ojos*. ¿Comprende? Up to your fuckin' eyeballs."

"I just wanted to let you know." Danny said meekly, relieved that Cubano's finger was the only thing aimed at his forehead. Danny wanted to leave while he still could, in one piece. Why had he come here without talking to his father first? He had acted on impulse, wanting to run far away from the club.

Cubano literally spit the words, "If you or your father lead them to me, there will be big trouble for you two. Big trouble. Don't forget, you were involved, if the cops don't take care of you, I will. ¿Comprende, *amigo*?"

Danny edged his way toward the door. "Don't worry. They won't get anything from us."

Once outside, Cubano's voice echoed in his head, "Trouble for you and your father. Big trouble."

CHAPTER 27

Wednesday, April 11th

Andy Scollari and I got to Crystal's funeral service early Wednesday morning. There were a few more people at Crystal's funeral than there were at Lola's the day before.

We showed the pictures to some of Crystal's friends before they went inside the church. We learned one or two first names and a nickname or two. One tall, thin girl identified Danny...first name again. "This chubby one in the pictures is Danny," she said. She wouldn't give us her name, though.

"Do you know Danny's last name?" I asked, not pushing her for her name, fearing she would stop talking to us.

She shrugged her shoulders. "No, sorry." She walked away and went inside the church.

A young man who was standing nearby volunteered, "Danny's got some kinda connection to an older guy in the Bronx. He'd get drugs from this guy."

"Do you know the guy's name?"

"No, only that he always has drugs and Danny uses him to get shit for people who go to his father's club."

"The club is on Trinity?" I asked.

Several friends gathered closer to us. Were they just curious about what we were doing there, or were they interested in how much we knew? I wondered.

"Have any of you been to Danny's father's club?"

Most shook their heads. Then one spoke for the small

group, "No, it's mostly for old men. People who have been there say the old guys creep them out. If any of us want any stuff — not heavy stuff — somebody gets word to Danny and he gets it."

The kids seemed to be getting uneasy. I figured I would try to get as much information as possible before they decided to take off. "Any of you know where Danny's connection lives?"

With that, the group began to break up and the kids turned to go into the church. The young man who first talked answered me, "Somewhere in the Bronx. Danny said the guy was a building super on DeKalb near Montefiore Hospital."

As he, too turned to walk away, Andy said to anyone left in earshot, "Please take one of my cards and call us if you think of something that might help us find this person."

"No way," one girl said more to her friends than to us, "we don't want to end up like Crystal and Lola."

CHAPTER 28

M rs. Ramos approached us after the funeral mass, "Thank you for coming today. I know you are trying hard to find out who did this thing to my baby. Are you coming to el cementerio?"

Andy looked at me while asking her, "I'm sorry, where?"

"Lo siento, the cemetery. I will give you coffee at my house after."

I thanked her. "No, we still have a lot of work to do. We want to follow up on the information we have as soon as possible." My heart broke again for her and for her husband, who stood quietly by her side.

Andy and I went back to headquarters and filled the lieutenant in on what we had learned. It wasn't much.

Capanno lit a cigarette. "You will have to wait a few days before you get back to the Bronx. I need you to cover the 4 – 12 shift for the rest of this week. Much as we need to solve this murder, we have other issues that need our attention. Getting back to the case he said, "Do you know where this club is that the kids were talking about?"

"It's not far from Crystal's mother's building. I'm sure we won't have trouble finding it."

Capanno turned to walk toward his office. "OK, I doubt it's going anywhere any time soon. Let's let the people there have some time to let down their guard, maybe think we're focused somewhere else."

Andy and I nodded in agreement with the lieutenant.

"Go down there next week." Capanno looked at Andy.

"Stay with Rocco, you two are well into the case together. I'll hold Smitty back a while after he gets back to work. You both know by now what a rough area this part of the Bronx is," exhaling some cigarette smoke. "No one there would hesitate to pop a cop."

I was anxious to get back to the Bronx, but I knew the lieutenant was right. We did have other cases. I had two burglaries to solve. Unfortunately, there wasn't much in the way of evidence or leads on them, so I needed to do some digging.

I tried to show interest in the cases despite my preoccupation with Lola and Crystal. "I'm waiting for the pawnshop list to come in to see if any of the stolen items were pawned." Capanno nodded and went into his office. Andy and I sat at our desks to get to work.

Andy looked at me and sounded surprised that I knew about working pawn shops, "I'm glad you know about that, Rocco. When someone pawns something, he has to show identification. As we all know, some of the criminals are not very bright and show their real ID. The more street-wise burglars sell to a fence, who specializes in moving stolen goods. Maybe you'll get lucky."

While I intended to give the burglary cases my full attention, I couldn't help thoughts about our murder victims and about our leads from running through my head. I wanted to solve my burglaries; I cared about the victims of those crimes. In all honesty, though, I was anxious to have the lieutenant let us get back to the Bronx. I wanted to prove that I had the skills to conduct a successful investigation of a crime of this magnitude.

Before leaving for the day, I said to Andy, "I'm not wishing any ill will on Smitty, but I'm glad I'm partnered with you."

"Me too you, Kid."

I followed Andy out the back door. It was the first time I had done that.

CHAPTER 29

Tuesday, April 17th

I arrived at headquarters before Andy. I was going over notes of the information we received from people at the funerals, when the phone rang.

"Detective Division, DeMarco."

"Rocco? It's Pete Swanson."

Detective Pete Swanson of the Mayville Police Department and I worked together in the tele-communications field.

"Hello Pete, how have you been?"

"I'm good. When did you make detective?"

"I'm only in the bureau as a P.O. for a short rotation. Silver said my sergeant promotion is coming soon. What's up?"

"We picked up a guy for burglary and some of the proceeds we recovered are from one of your department's burglaries."

"That's great Pete. What did he have?

"Some jewelry. One item was a college ring from Fordham University. I thought that was a unique item so I checked the sheets from other PDs and it matched an item from your burglary."

"Thanks, let us know when you are done with the guy and we will pick him up. At the very least, we can hit him with possession of stolen property. You just helped me close one of my cases, I'm afraid the Thompson burglary is cold."

"No problem Rocco let me know when the sergeant thing happens and we'll go celebrate with a beer."

"You got it."

I was ready to get back to our murder investigation.

Andy wasn't in the habit of arriving early – or on time. When he did arrive, he was holding two cups of coffee that he had picked up on his way in. Handing one to me he said, "Rocco, what time do you want to leave?" He, too, was ready to get to our investigation.

Thanks for the coffee, Andy. I think we should wait 'til after rush hour," I was finishing up the supplemental burglary forms. "Should be less traffic and easier to find this social club. Mrs. Ramos said it's only a couple of blocks from her apartment. I hope getting there in the morning will give us a chance of finding someone in. You want to drive or do you want me to drive?"

Andy moved toward the sign-out sheet beside the cabinet that held the keys to our department vehicles. "You can drive, Kid." He tossed a set of keys to me. "You're more familiar with where we're going than I am."

"OK," I agreed. "I see we're taking our customized Bronx car – the one without hubcaps." We both laughed as we headed out, taking our coffees with us.

We made good time to the Bronx and found the corner on which we believed the club was located. We were able to find a parking spot near the corner, where there would be less chance of getting boxed in if we had to get the hell out of there. The club was supposedly inside a building that resembled a small warehouse. We located a basement entrance.

"You think this is the place, Rocco?"

"Were you expecting a neon sign flashing, *Illegal Social Club*?

Andy laughed.

We approached the door without hurry; we did not want to call attention to ourselves. The wooden door had a small opening at eye level to allow occupants to screen the clientele. I glanced at Andy.

"Were you expecting a doorbell?" He joked.

I knocked three or four times before we heard some noise from inside.

After a few minutes, a young, chubby-faced man came to the door and looked out at us through the opening.

"Who are you and what do you want?" He said through the square space. He spoke with unconvincing authority.

This had to be Danny. From what we had heard, he was a bit of a dim wit. The way he sounded reinforced that description.

"We're police officers," Andy said. "We need to ask you some questions."

"Do you have a warrant?"

"A *warrant*?" I whispered.

"This guy's a real idiot. He's been watching too many episodes of *Hill Street Blues*," Andy said, rolling his eyes. "He thinks we need a warrant to ask him a few questions."

"We don't need a warrant," I answered him. "We just want to ask you some questions." I gave him a cold stare through the hole. "Do you want to open the door and let us in, or do you want us to get that warrant and come back with more cops to search this place from corner to corner? I'm sure that NYPD would love to take a good look around."

Danny opened the door and let us in. He was no longer acting like such a tough guy. "You guys from the 4-1?"

"No, we're from the Lakeside Police Department" Andy said, showing him his badge.

Squinting at the badge Danny said, "Where the fuck is that, New Jersey?"

Here we go again. "You folks need to venture out of the Bronx every now and then. No, it's in Westchester County. And if you ask if Lakeside is *upstate*, I'm going to cuff you, drive you to Buffalo and let you walk back from there. We'll show you where upstate really is."

"Um, OK, sorry. So, why're you in the Bronx?"

"Are you Danny?" Andy asked, moving things along.

"Yeah," and then he paused. "How did you know my name?"

"We'll ask the questions if you don't mind," I said, "however, we learned your name at the funeral services for two girls from here who were found in Lakeside, murdered."

Danny was getting flustered. "What girls?"

I pulled out a chair. "Sit down."

Danny's face was flushed. He watched Andy strolling around his filthy club, looking at the bar, the tables, the debris from the previous night still on the floor.

"What's your last name?"

"Varanda?"

You're not sure of your last name?" I asked him. This is your father's club, right? What's his name?"

Danny's eyes continued to follow Andy. "Pablo." He pointed at Andy, "I thought you said you weren't here about the club. What's he looking for?"

"We aren't interested in this club right now. We're investigating a homicide."

Danny looked afraid. "A what?"

I looked at him coldly, starting to lose patience, "Homicide! Murder! You know, the girls who were killed."

"So, why're you asking me?" He continued to watch Andy, "You think two girls were murdered here?" He was clearly nervous.

"We don't know where they were killed, but they ended up in our town and we traced them back to the Bronx."

Danny's facial expressions and tone amped from concern when we talked about the club to panic when we mentioned the murders.

"So, you're here because some girls you think I knew are dead?"

"We don't *think* you knew them; we saw pictures of you with them. We *know* you knew them. We wouldn't be here if we believed you didn't know them and didn't know they were dead."

Andy stopped walking around. "You think we're stupid?"

Danny gulped, "No, I don't think you're stupid." He stood up. "I'm just not sure why cops from upstate would be down in the Bronx asking..."

"Sit down. I told you, we're from Westchester."

"I guess you wanna walk home from Buffalo," Andy said coldly.

"Both girls were from the Bronx. We are trying to find out who might know something about their deaths. We don't know where they were killed, but *they were both from the Bronx*," I emphasized, "so that seemed the logical place to start. Understand?"

"OK, Detective," Danny put his hands up as if to say, *hold it*. "So, why'd you come to me?"

"One of the girls, Crystal Ramos, had a lot of pictures of you, so I figured you must know her pretty well."

"Crystal is one of the dead girls?" He feigned surprise. "You said two girls. Who was the other one?"

"Lola Vasquez. Did you know her, too?"

"Oh, man, Yeah, Crystal and Lola hung around together."

"Did they ever hang out together here at this club?"

"Who? Crystal and Lola?"

"Are you fucking with me or are you just stupid? Yes, Crystal and Lola."

Danny's lips quivered. "Yeah, maybe once or twice." His eyes darted to see what Andy was doing. "I can't remember the last time they were here."

"You expect us to believe your memory is that bad? Wasn't Crystal a little young to be in this place?" I didn't give him a chance to answer, "We understand they were planning on having some sort of party here." I learned this during my conversation with Mrs. Ramos. Crystal had been talking about it with her on the night they left for the club to make the arrangements.

Danny looked up as if trying to get his brain to work, "Oh

yeah, yeah... now I remember. Lola was going into the Navy or Army or something. That's the reason Crystal came in."

"When was it they came in to arrange the party?"

Seemingly straining his brain, "I think it was a few weeks ago or maybe longer."

"Did they have the party?" I knew the answer, but was interested in what Danny might admit.

"No," shaking his head, "I would have known. I do all the setting up, not my father."

"When will your father be here?"

"He should be in later. He stays here pretty late at night when his older friends come in, so he sleeps in the morning. The girls never came in when the older guys were here. The older guys would hit on them, and the more the men got drunk, the more they upset some of the girls."

What a place for young girls to have a party, I thought to myself. I said, "OK, we'll want to speak with him. Tell him that." I looked the place over. "So, when you say you were the one *setting up the party*, what exactly does that mean?"

Andy quickly threw in more questions, "Was there going to be a band? Were you going to have food? Were you going to throw a fresh coat of paint on this lovely place?"

I glared at Danny. "What exactly did you need to *set up*?"

Andy loomed over him. "Was there going to be drinking?"

We were hitting him with questions so fast that he didn't have time to think about what he was saying. "I was going to set them up with a little coke. But they were going to bring their own booze." He had spoken without thinking.

"A little *coke*," Andy repeated with a smile, "like *Coca Cola*?"

I leaned into him. "You expect us to believe that you were setting them up to get soda pop?"

"No, um," he sputtered nervously, "...you know, some drug stuff."

"And, just where would you get this drug stuff?" Andy was on a roll. He had this kid answering without thinking.

"I have a guy I know that I can buy stuff from." Danny was looking back and forth from Andy to me, not sure of who he should talk to. "Not a lot of stuff. Just a couple of nickel bags."

I jumped back in, "And who is this guy you get your stuff from? Does he come here?"

"No, I don't think he's ever been here. I go to his building."

"You don't *think* or you don't *know*?" I fired.

Without giving him time to answer, Andy asked, "...and where might that building be?"

"DeKalb. I think he's a building super there."

I lean into his space. "Again, you *think*? You go to him to buy drugs and you don't know if he's the super or not? You *think* you know his name? *Where* on DeKalb?"

"You guys know how to find DeKalb?"

I nodded. "Yeah, city boy, we can find DeKalb. What's the guy's name?

"I only know him by his nickname. They call him *Cubano*. He's from Cuba."

"And how old is this guy?"

"I'm not sure." He points at Andy and says, "Maybe not as old as him," then he pointed at me, "but older than you."

Just when he thought we might be leaving, I said, "Let's take a ride over there together to meet this Cubano."

Danny could no longer hide his panic. His face paled. He clearly did not want to go with us to Cubano. "I don't know if he's there. I only go there once in a while. He hardly knows me. We should wait. Or you can go without me." Danny was stammering, his voice rising.

I smiled and looked straight into his eyes. "You said he's a building super, right? What good is a building super if he isn't there to take care of the building? Why are you stalling? Is he going to tell us something you don't want us to know?"

Beads of sweat formed on Danny's forehead. "No, I just

need to stay here to watch the club until my father comes in. I'm in charge," he said weakly, all hints of authority gone.

"We're sure everything will be fine until your dad comes in. Do you drive?"

"Um, yeah, I got a car, but my father's using it." Danny hoped that would enable him to stay behind.

He was wrong.

"That's Ok," I said. "We'll take our car."

CHAPTER 30

On the ride to DeKalb, Danny sat in the back seat of our Bronx-mobile, squirming and sweating. If body language was a reliable indicator, this kid was worried and scared.

DeKalb Avenue is a short street at the rear of the Montefiore Medical Center, which takes up a full city block. DeKalb intersects with Gun Hill Road, which is close to the Bronx River Parkway. If we didn't feel like driving this kid back to his club, we could always leave him with his buddy Cubano and jump on the Parkway for an easy drive home.

We parked, got out of the car, and walked toward the front door of the building. Cubano's building was twelve stories; it didn't look as run down as some of the buildings we had been in up to this point.

"No," Danny stopped us as we neared the door, "don't go in that way. His apartment is in the basement. You go in through this alley on the side." Danny went on ahead.

We followed him down the alley. I noticed bags of trash lined up along the wall of the building; the bags resembled the ones our victims were in when they were found.

"These bags look familiar to you?" I whispered to Andy.

Andy shrugged his shoulders, "I don't know. I suppose all trash bags look alike."

We entered the building through a side door and found ourselves in a dark, open basement. I began to feel uncomfortable right away. "Where's this guy's apartment?"

"Keep walking straight," Danny said, pointing. "His door is this way."

"He's the super?" Andy asked. "And he doesn't have working lights down here?"

Fortunately, there was some daylight coming in from the doorway and a small window that faced the alley. This was not a place you'd want to be in at night.

"Wait here, outside the door." Danny said. "I'll see if he's home."

Both Andy and I thought that Danny intended to warn this Cubano guy that the cops were right outside. We didn't want to let the kid out of our sight in the dark basement, and we didn't know if Cubano would bolt out another door. There proved to be no need to worry: Danny turned from the apartment door and said, "OK, he's home. You can come in."

We entered and were in a disheveled, shabby apartment. It was dark, clammy, and it smelled foul. "This guy must be a great super," I said, quietly, to Andy.

Cubano was definitely not happy to see us; in fact, he looked as though he would delight in killing us right then and there.

"Hello, sir," I began respectfully, not wanting to ignite a spark. "I am Officer Rocco DeMarco. This gentleman is Detective Andrew Scollari. We're conducting an investigation and would like to ask you some questions, if we may."

Cubano's scowl remained. He threw a quick, angry stare at Danny. "What kind of investigation? What precinct are you from?"

"We are not NYPD," I said. "We're from the Lakeside Police Department."

"What the hell is the Lakeside Police Department?" He looked at the badge Andy produced.

"What is that, upstate?"

"Lakeside is a police agency in Westchester County." I answered evenly.

"What kind of investigation brings two cops from upstate Westchester to the Bronx? And more importantly, to me?"

"We'll get to the purpose of our visit after you answer a couple of questions. What is your full name?"

"Ernesto Malino. Is that enough information for you to give me the reason that you are here?"

Cubano was irritated. We were dealing with a man who appeared to be accustomed to using intimidation and fear. We weren't going to let him think we were susceptible to either.

I noticed a tattoo in the web of his hand between his thumb and forefinger. I could, when I glanced at him, see that Andy had seen it, too.

We had recently attended a seminar at the Police Academy about how certain tattoos denote criminal status and gang affiliation. Cubano's marking indicated that he had been a violent criminal in Cuba.

"Mr. Malino," I asked, "are you a *Marielito*?" This was the name given to Cubans who emigrated to the United States during the Mariel Boatlift in 1980. Several of those released to the United States were violent criminals.

Cubano's expression turned even more sinister. "Yes. I came here in 1980."

"Your English is very good," I said.

"Yes, it is," he snapped without comment.

"Were you ever in prison in Cuba?" Inmates in Cuba were often tattooed with numbers inside their bottom lip. "May I see the inside of your bottom lip?"

He clenched his fist but complied. When he rolled his lip, there was no tattoo. "Now," he said forcefully and smugly, "tell me why you are here in my house."

"We are investigating the murder of two Bronx girls. Their bodies were found in our town, Lakeside," I said.

He glared at Danny. We had hit a nerve.

"Mind if we sit down?"

Andy found a seat and asked Cubano, "Do you live here by yourself?"

"Yes. It is just me. Any family I have left is still in Cuba. What do the murders of two girls have to do with me?"

Andy ignored the question. "What kind of things do you have to do as the super?"

"Take out garbage, fix little things, shit like that."

Knowing full well this man must have been involved in more than fixing apartments, Andy asked, "What did you do in Cuba?"

Cubano hesitated for a moment. "Why do you ask me what I did in Cuba?"

"Just trying to see why you left and how it was that you came to be in this job here in the Bronx."

Cubano shot a look at me then looked back to Andy. "I did odd jobs. Why do you care so much about me?"

Andy continued to question Cubano. I looked around the room. We were in what I supposed was his living room, off the entrance foyer. I couldn't help but think that this must have been a really nice basement apartment back in the day. Although I could only see the foyer and living room, I could tell there were other rooms, making this a big apartment.

Then something caught my eye.

There was a piece of twine about a foot long with loops at each end being used to hold back drapes that separated the living room from the foyer. The twine looked *exactly* like the twine that had been tied around the wrist of one of our victims.

Andy had wrapped up his questioning without learning much more that would help us and without escalating the anger that Cubano was obviously feeling. We thanked *Mr. Malino* for his time and cooperation and told him to contact us if he thought of anything that might help us with our investigation. Never once had he asked about the dead girls.

As Andy and I were about to leave, we noticed a shelf on the wall in the foyer. On it were a couple of boxes of green plastic trash bags and a large roll of twine.

I hesitated at the door and turned back. "Mr. Malino, can we have a couple of those bags and a section of twine?"

"Why?" he snapped, more than anxious to have us leave.

I shrugged. "Nothing important," I did not want to heighten his suspicions of what we may or may not have known. "We have some junk in the trunk of our car. When I saw the trash bags, I remembered that we said we would clean things up before we returned the car."

Cubano shot me an ominous glare and ripped two bags from one of the boxes. Clearly annoyed and wanting to just get us out of his apartment he said, "How much rope do you want?" He was being complicit, if not friendly.

"Just a short piece, if you can spare it."

Cubano produced an alarmingly large knife, cut a piece of the twine and gave it to me.

I looked over at Danny, who stood nervously in the rear corner of the living room. He looked as if he was about to faint. "C'mon Danny, you're leaving with us."

It was not a comfortable walk from the apartment back through the alley, to the car. We could feel Cubano watching us, making sure we walked directly out to the car.

Once out of earshot, Danny almost shrieked, "What the fuck were all those questions about? You were treating him like you suspected him of something. Why'd you ask for trash bags?"

"Didn't you hear me, we need them for trash."

"Get in the car," Andy said to Danny.

I turned from the front seat to look back, directly at Danny, "Did you notice he never once asked who the girls were, or how they were killed?"

Danny looked down and said nothing.

"You know what I think, Danny?"

"What?" he mumbled.

"If we had left you with Cubano, we'd be investigating your homicide next."

CHAPTER 31

As soon as we got back to headquarters, I walked into Lieutenant Capanno's office. "Hey, Lieu, I think Andy and I made some progress this morning."

Capanno looked up from his paperwork. "Tell me."

"We're pretty sure we were at the location of the killings."

He took his reading glasses off, "What happened? When you left here you were headed to that social club in the Bronx. You think the girls were killed there?"

"That kid, Danny, gave up his drug dealer, a guy called *Cubano*. We had the kid take us over to Cubano's basement apartment on DeKalb. We spotted evidence that seemed too coincidental to be...coincidental. We think the girls were killed there."

Capanno lit a cigarette. "What'd you spot?"

"There was twine holding Cubano's drapes..."

Capanno rocked back in his chair, interested. "Go on."

"Remember the picture of the twine I took at the morgue? It was tied around the wrists of one of the girls."

"Yeah, I remember that."

I grabbed a piece of paper and a pen and leaned onto his desk; I made a sketch of the twine that was on the victim. "Remember? That's what it looked like. Look at the knot."

"Yeah, I remember."

"The twine on Cubano's drapes was identical, same length, same oval ends, tied just like the knot." Do you think that can be a coincidence?"

Capanno looked hard at the sketch. "Probably not," he nodded.

Capanno looked past me and called out the door. "Andy, come in here." Andy appeared at the office door. "Did you see this piece of twine?"

"Yeah Lieu. We brought a piece back with us that we can use for comparison."

"You took the piece off his drapes?" Capanno asked, raising his eyebrows.

"No Lieu, we got a different piece."

I explained. "When we saw the piece of twine and some trash bags that seemed to be the same as the ones in which the girls were found, we asked Cubano to give us some twine and a trash bag we thought we could use as evidence to nail him for the murders, and he complied." I smiled and winked at Andy.

"Are you fucking kidding me? Tell me what really happened!"

"Lieu, as we were walking down the alley to this guy's apartment, we saw bags of trash lined up against the side of the building. They looked like the ones our victims were found in. As we were leaving the apartment, we saw the same bags and then the twine on a shelf. Rocco asked Cubano if we could have two bags and some twine because we had garbage in our trunk that we wanted to bag up."

"And the asshole bought that load of shit?"

"He couldn't refuse to give us the stuff; he'd look like he was hiding something."

"You realize we can't use any of it as evidence," Capanno said. "We didn't have a warrant."

"We didn't conduct a search for them," I said. "The bags and twine were plainly visible. I realize most trash bags look alike, but the ones we saw certainly resembled ours. We took a shot and asked for the stuff and Cubano gave it to us. He really didn't have a choice."

Andy added, "Like Rocco said, Lieu, we didn't search for anything. It was all in plain sight. We simply asked if we could have them."

The lieutenant was concerned about using these items as evidence. Can we use them to confirm our suspicions without entering them as evidence?" I asked.

Lieutenant Capanno leaned back in his chair again and lit a cigarette. He stared at the smoke as if in the smoke he was going to see the answer. "Yeah, I guess we can do that. If we get a warrant, I want that piece holding the drapes listed specifically. It was in plain view, right?"

"Yes, it was," I answered. "It's not as if he was trying to hide it. I don't think he even saw me looking at it."

The lieutenant was not convinced, but continued, "Where do you two go from here?"

"Andy and I thought we would give it a couple of days and then drop back in on Danny. We believe that he was either involved in the murders or knows who committed them. We also want to speak to his father; Danny probably didn't do anything on his own. His father is more than likely involved in this, too."

"OK. Rocco, you write up what you two have so far. I'll give the DA a call and explain the progress we've made. I'll ask his advice on how best to proceed. I don't want to do anything that might compromise our case... Anymore!"

I could tell that the lieutenant was still concerned about our collection of rope and garbage bags. We might not be able to introduce them as evidence, but taking them served to let Danny and Cubano know we were on to them.

A short time later, Capanno came out of his office. "I just had a conversation with the ADA assigned to our case, John Bishop. He told me there's probably no problem with the items that were given voluntarily."

"Is there anything we can use the two items for, Lieu, without putting them forward as evidence?" I asked.

"We can send them to the FBI lab for comparison. They already have the bags we sent for prints: they might be able to tell us if we're in the right ballpark."

The FBI also had a piece of twine and could examine the two samples to see if they were the same. The examination of the twine could be compared for construction, color, composition, and diameter.

Capanno stood up and poured himself some coffee. "If we find there is a link, we could get a search warrant for the rest of that apartment." Then he added emphatically, "Don't get anything else without a warrant."

I was worried that Capanno thought that I made an over-zealous decision similar to one Detective Smith made when he took the victim's clothes from the Medical Examiner's Office. Smitty didn't ask anyone. He simply took the clothes and possibly compromised evidence.

Evidence has to have a documented chain of possession. The appropriate course of action would have been for Smitty to receive the clothes from the M.E., sign for them and then enter them as evidence at headquarters. That way, the possession of these items could be documented at every step. The way Smitty took them clearly compromised the items as evidence.

I imagined how the cross examination of Smitty's actions would go during the trial:

"Detective Smith, where did you get these items of clothing?"

"From the M.E.'s office."

"Did the M.E. give them to you and document that on the evidence chain of custody sheet?"

"No, I just figured he was done with them and we could take them."

"So, you 'just figured' you would stuff them in a bag, like someone raiding a Goodwill box?"

It would be hard, if not impossible, for Detective Smith to answer questions without making himself look like an inept fool.

That is exactly what Capanno feared I had done as well. And exactly what I feared a defense attorney would do to me.

CHAPTER 32

Wednesday, April 18th

I wrote my reports to document the actions we had taken to date. I wanted to be careful not to leave anything out, so I included such things as facial expressions and body language of the people we questioned.

Before we returned to the Bronx, I made sure I was not short-changing my other investigations. Once I knew everything was in order, I thought about our upcoming interviews; I was especially curious about meeting Pablo Varanda, Danny's father.

It would be interesting to see how the elder Varanda would respond to our questioning. Would he panic, the way his son did, or would he remain cool and seemingly disinterested?

My enthusiasm about getting back to the Bronx was dashed when Smitty breezed in and greeted me with, "Hey Kid, I'm back. What's on the agenda?"

I tried to hide my disappointment about not continuing my partnership with Andy. "Good to see you're back, Glen. You and I will be teamed up and headed to a social club in the Bronx to talk to some suspects. I'll fill you in on the way."

I wasn't only concerned about my safety in the Bronx with Smitty as my backup, I was equally, if not more concerned with Smitty's lack of professionalism and investigative recklessness.

I popped my head into the lieutenant's office to let Capanno know we were leaving. "We're heading out, Lieu."

"Remember what I said to you once before, Rocco. Don't let Smitty do anything without you."

"Got it, Lieu."

When we got to the car, I said, "The club's on Trinity Avenue, not far from where the girls were from. I can tell you the easiest way to get there."

"That's OK Kid, I'm sure I can find it. We gotta make a quick stop first."

"First things first," he said as he pulled up to a luncheonette. "I need to get something to eat. You hungry?"

"I'm good, maybe just a cup of coffee." I was impatient, but was not going to start the day off with a scowl or an argument. I would try to enjoy some coffee while Smitty indulged in a full breakfast.

We finally headed for the Bronx. To my amazement, Smitty didn't get lost

"You found the street pretty quick; I'm impressed."

"OK, Kid," he said, pleased with the compliment. "What's the number?"

"I don't know if this place has a number, Glen, but it's on the corner of 161st and Trinity."

We parked, but not, I thought, close enough to the building to allow one of us to keep an eye on the car.

A brisk walk brought us to the door to the club; after we knocked, the small window opened and, as before, Danny stuck his face against the screen. He didn't recognize Glen.

"Who is it?"

"It's Detective Smith. Open the door, you little shit."

What a great way to start our interview.

Although his large frame blocked my view of Danny, I decided to speak up before Smitty could say anything else. "Danny, it's Officer DeMarco with Detective Smith."

Danny opened the door and we stepped into the South Bronx's popular, albeit illegal social club.

Smitty looked around. "Holy shit, what the hell kind of a

shithole is this?" He turned to Danny. "Were you afraid we were the building department? This place looks like it should be condemned."

I cringed.

Danny just stared at Smitty. "What do you guys want?"

"Danny, this gentleman is a detective." Glen liked it when you called him *detective*.

"Glen, Danny's father is the owner of this club."

In deference to his seniority, I let Smitty ask the questions. He *was* the detective.

"Is your father here, Junior?"

Danny gave me a quizzical look as if to ask, *Who the fuck is this guy?* He looked back at Smitty. "Yes, he's in the back room, I'll get him."

Danny and his father walked from the back room together. Smitty postured, "I'm Detective Smith. Do you speak English?"

Pablo, gave Smitty a critical once-over before he answered, "Yes. Who did you say you were?"

"I'm Detective Smith. Got it, Mister?"

Pablo took a step back. "Can I see your badge? Please?"

Thankfully, Danny eased the escalating tension. "It's OK, Papa, the other officer was here before and he identified himself then. They're real cops."

"You bet your ass we're real cops," Smitty just couldn't let up. "I'm in charge here. What's your full name?"

Pablo looked at me. "Pablo Varanda."

"Look at me when I'm talking to you," Smitty continued to incense the owner. "And this is your club?"

"Yes, Officer, this is my place."

"That's *Detective*! We're here investigating the murder of two girls, Lola Vasquez and Crystal Ramos. These two girls came to your club to see Danny before they disappeared. They wanted to have a party?"

"Yes, *Detective*, that's what they said. One of them was going into the Army or something."

Satisfied that his rank had been acknowledged, "And you took your son, and the girls to this Cuban guy's house for what reason?"

Pablo shrugged his shoulders, "They wanted some drugs, not much, for their party."

"And this Cuban guy is who you go to for *grugs*?"

Pablo looked at Danny. "¿Qué es *grugs*?"

I said, "*Drugs*, Sir, he's asking about *drugs*."

"Sí. I went with my son and the girls to make sure they didn't get ripped off. I went to keep everybody safe. I had never gone there before...we're not los traficantes de drogas."

Danny detected the look of confusion on Smitty's face and said, "he said we aren't drug dealers Detective."

"Relax Pablo, we aren't narcs, we don't give a shit about your so-called club, legal or otherwise. We're investigating a murder. That's all we give a shit about."

Pablo looked at Danny again and nodded, signaling that he could explain.

Danny looked uneasy. "I'm the one who goes to see Cubano every now and then when I want a little coke. I don't sell it. I just use it or get it for friends. That's what we brought Lola and Crystal there for."

Smitty turned to Pablo. "And you went with your son this time, but never went before?"

"Yes. Like I said, I didn't want them to get ripped off. I also didn't want Danny and the girls alone with this man until I checked things out."

"So, what happened when you all got to this guy's house?" Glen turned to me and asked, "Where'd you say this was, Rocco, by Montefiore Hospital?"

I nodded, "On DeKalb."

"We brought the girls in and Cubano said he would take care of them. Me and my father left because the girls said they could get home on their own. Cubano seemed cool and the girls were OK."

Smitty looked at Pablo. "Sounds like you were really concerned about them. So, did they ever come back here for the party?"

Danny looked down at the floor and shook his head, "No, that was the last time I saw them."

"And you didn't think that was strange?" Smitty asked. "That they were planning a party, wanted some *'grugs'* for it, and never showed up to have the party? And then you say you never saw them again?"

"We figured Lola left for the Army before they could have the party," Danny answered.

"And what about Crystal? Did you think she went into the Army, too?"

"Crystal was younger than Lola. I figured that when Lola left, Crystal found kids more her age to hang out with. She never came to the club without Lola, anyway."

Smitty glared at him. "And now she never will."

I had to admit that Glen was getting them nervous with his questions. That said, we were no closer to knowing what happened to the girls.

"OK Kid, let's get out of here. They don't know shit."

I didn't agree. I suspected that Danny and Pablo knew a lot more, but I was in no position to question the detective's decision.

After we left, Glen found a place in Eastchester to get some lunch. The man's appetite was insatiable.

When we got back to headquarters, I wrote my report and then went to talk with the lieutenant. "Smitty did most of the talking, Lieu. He didn't get us much closer to any specific answers, but he did shake them up. I didn't leave his side; I could, if needed, testify to whatever information comes of this interview."

Capanno lit a cigarette and said, "Thank you. I'm sure you learned some interesting interview techniques from our seasoned detective."

I turned and chuckled. "I sure did."

We both laughed and I left the office.

CHAPTER 33

I was about to call it a day when Lieutenant Capanno called me into his office. "Rocco, come in and close the door."

The lieutenant put one cigarette out and lit another; this was not a good sign.

"Did I screw something up, Lieu?"

"No, you're OK, Rocco. You probably aren't going to like what I have to tell you. I asked Chief Silver to put Glen on something else and partner you and Andy. It appears as though we are getting very close in this case and I cringe at the thought of Smitty doing something he might have to account for or worse yet, testify to." Capanno looked up and exhaled some smoke. "The chief said he has to keep Detective Smith with you because he is more senior than Andy. Not to mention, he would throw a shit fit being taken off a case of this magnitude."

I was relieved that Capanno didn't tell me that I was being taken off the case. If it meant being with Smitty, so be it. "I often find him amusing, Lieu, and with this case, I can use a little comic relief every now and then. Don't worry."

Capanno smiled. "Thanks, Rocco."

"I think Smitty likes being partnered with me on this case. I doubt he wants to go to the Bronx by himself, and I think he feels safe with me. And I know he likes to boss me around because I have a *silver* shield."

Seeing that I was OK with the arrangement, Capanno sat back in his chair. "What do you have planned next, after your last visit with Danny and his father?"

"I thought we could stake out Cubano's apartment to see who comes and goes. I would be interested in seeing whether or not Danny or his father visits his place, and if they do, how often."

Capanno nodded, seeming to like the idea. "I'm curious about how're you going to do this without raising suspicion? The only vantage point seems to be from the street or the hospital."

"I think we are in luck Lieu, there are hospital workers picketing on the sidewalk right across the street from Cubano's building."

Capanno leaned forward, his eyes widened, "You're not suggesting we put Smitty on the sidewalk and make him march around for a couple of hours, are you?"

I laughed. "No, Lieu, while he could use the exercise, his idea of a stakeout is to park the police car right in front of the building."

Lieutenant Capanno put his hands behind his head, "So tell me, how are you going to do this with Smitty?"

"Actually, I was thinking I could blend in nicely with the hospital workers. From what I've seen, they're mostly younger people; Smitty would stand out like a sore thumb. He can park farther down the street. As long as he brings enough food, he'll be happy to sit there, eat and see if anyone of interest passes by."

"Sounds like a good idea, Rocco. Remember to let Smitty feel that he's in charge."

"Not to worry," I said. "I'd sure like to get a couple of pictures of who goes into Cubano's apartment, but no picket-line worker would be taking pictures of the building across the street. I would rather Smitty was not too close, but close enough to get some shots. I'm just not sure that he can operate the 35mm camera."

"Which camera do you think he's capable of operating?" Capanno was leaning on his elbows waiting for my suggestion.

"Could you just see him out there with the old Graflex? He'd look like Matthew Brady taking Civil War photos."

"Maybe we can give Glen the 35mm Lieu, and see if he'll give a try."

"OK," Capanno said, "See what you can do."

I left in search of Smitty. He was getting some coffee to enjoy with some doughnuts. "What do you think about staking out Cubano's apartment? Maybe get some pictures of anyone who goes in or out?"

Smitty rubbed the back of his neck. "How're we going to do this, Kid?"

"I thought of a way we could watch the apartment from across the street. The hospital workers are picketing and no one would notice one additional picketer."

He shook his head vigorously. "Oh, hell no! There's no way in hell I'm walking a picket line."

"I'll do the picket line. You stay in the car. The lieutenant is letting us take the 35mm camera; maybe you can get some pictures from where you're parked. You know, faces or license plates."

"I hate that fucking camera."

Picking up the 35mm camera, I said, "Well, the Graflex doesn't have a telephoto lens. If you got close enough to use the Graflex, someone would see you. I can give you a quick lesson on this one if you want."

"Photography is your thing Kid, not mine, but we can see about trying." Smitty looked at the camera the way a youngster would look at growling dog.

Although I doubted that Smitty would actually try to get some pictures, I did give him a reasonable tutorial on the use of the camera. One could always hope.

"So, Detective Smith, when do you think we should get back to Cubano's?" I needed to fully restore his sense of authority.

"I'm off tomorrow Kid. Why don't you catch up on your reports and think about how you are going to blend in with the hospital workers. Maybe you can wear a stethoscope. Ha ha!"

"Don't worry, I'll blend. The lieutenant wants me to take tomorrow off too, so let's do this Friday."

"OK Kid, see you then. I'll be in after breakfast."

I laughed to myself and left for the day.

CHAPTER 34

Friday, April 20th

G len arrived Friday morning, almost on time.
"G'morning, Glen. We can leave whenever you're ready.
I'm all set. I have the camera in case you want to give it a try." I
felt sure that we were not going to get any pictures from Smitty.

"Yeah, maybe I'll give it a shot, Kid."

We went out to the car and I got right into the passen-
ger's seat. As we pulled out of the lot, I could tell we were once
again heading in the direction of the luncheonette.

"I get hungry Kid, I may not find a good place to get food
down there. We'll stop for a quick bite."

"As long as we're stopping, I'll get a coffee." I had my one
and only breakfast for the day at home.

After Glen's breakfast, we headed for Cubano's apartment
on DeKalb Avenue. DeKalb was right off Gun Hill Road, which
was off the Bronx River Parkway. It was easy to get to.

We found parking on Kossuth Avenue, which ran paral-
lel to DeKalb and intersected at a fork just south of Cubano's
apartment building.

"This looks like a good spot Glen." I took the camera and
pointed it in the direction of Cubano's building. "You may be
able to get some shots from here."

"Let me see that thing, Kid." Glen took the camera and
looked at it as if he had never seen it before. "Does it have
film?"

"All loaded; just look through the viewfinder and push that button," I pointed to the black button next to the finder. Smitty nodded and put the camera down.

The stakeout location was close enough to Cubano's building, but not close enough to attract attention to our unmarked police car. This location also gave a good line of sight to the target building, which would allow identification of people walking down the alley or of vehicles pulling up to the front. The only reason a person would have for walking down that alley was to enter Cubano's apartment. This made our surveillance easier; we could focus on anyone in the alley instead of on the busier front door foot traffic. With a telephoto lens, it would be possible for Smitty to get clear shots of people and cars coming and going. Possible, not probable.

I left Smitty in the parked car and walked over to the picket line in front of the hospital. I approached one of the people holding a sign that read, TREAT YOUR WORKERS FAIRLY. "Is there someone in charge I can talk to?"

The worker looked me over and figured I didn't look like someone who was going to cause problems. He pointed to a man farther up the sidewalk and said, "His name's Ralph, he's the one you want to see."

I took out my badge and ID as I approached the individual identified as Ralph. "Hello, are you Ralph? My name is Officer DeMarco from the Lakeside Police Department."

"What brings Westchester police to this little slice of heaven, Officer?"

"Ralph, you're one of the few people here in the Bronx, who doesn't consider anything north of here to be upstate."

"You're right I'm from Eastchester."

I chuckled. "Call me Rocco, Ralph. We're down here looking for a guy who may live in the building across the street." I pointed at Cubano's building.

"What do you mean we? Are there other officers from your department here as well?"

"Just my partner, a detective parked up the road. We didn't want to attract attention with a police vehicle."

Ralph laughed. "Like a police car would be an unusual sight down here."

"I have a favor to ask. Would you mind if I walk the line with your workers so I can keep an eye on that building without looking out of place?"

"Sure, you can. The more people carrying signs the better. I'll even give you one of our paper hats with the union label on it."

I smiled and nodded, "Thank you."

"You fit right in," he said, handing me the hat. "If you tell me what this guy looks like, I can keep an eye out, too, and let you know if I see someone matching his description entering or exiting the building."

As much as I appreciated Ralph's offer, I did not want to let him know too many specifics. "Thanks, Ralph, but I've got this."

I walked the picket line, keeping the alley leading to Cubano's apartment in view. After almost two hours, during which there was a change of shift for the hospital workers on the picket line, I observed two men enter the alley. They appeared to be Hispanic males, late 20's or 30's. I didn't notice them emerge from a vehicle, so I assumed they came by foot from the direction of Gun Hill Road, opposite from where Smitty was parked. About 20 minutes later, I saw Danny drive up in his beat-up yellow car.

Danny parked and walked down the alley. Another hour passed before Danny and the other two men appeared in the alley together. Danny got in his car; sure enough, the other two walked up the street toward Gun Hill Road. I wasn't sure if they had a car up there or were using public transportation.

I looked at my watch and walked over to Ralph. "I guess no luck today; maybe our guy works. I'm going to call it quits. Thanks for letting me blend. How long are you guys going to be here?"

"We just started. The hospital doesn't seem in any rush to listen to us. I imagine that we will be here for a while."

"Do you picket on weekends?"

"Yeah. Not as many people show, but we'll be here."

"Thank you. We'll be back, too, probably tomorrow, even though it's Saturday."

"I'll see you, then. I'm shop steward. I have to keep these folks motivated," he smiled.

"OK. Can I hang on to the hat?"

"If you like it that much, you can keep it."

I walked down the street to meet Glen and fill him in on what I was able to observe.

Detective Smith was pleased that we were finished for the day. "See anything worthwhile, Kid?"

"I recognized Danny and his car; there were two other guys who went down the alley just before he did. I've never seen them before."

"Was the kid's old man with him?"

"No, and I'm wondering if whatever he's doing is something his father is unaware of. When he was around his father, he made it sound as though he didn't come here often and here he is, a couple of days after we spoke. I told the union shop steward we'd be back tomorrow."

Smitty started to shake his head. "*You'll* be back tomorrow, Kid. I don't do weekends."

I wasn't sure how he was going to tell the lieutenant he wouldn't be coming down with me. In any event, I welcomed the news that I'd be without him.

We headed back to headquarters after making a brief stop at our local deli; Smitty was starving, of course. I was hungry, too, after the hours on the picket line.

The lieutenant was waiting for us. I filled him in on the morning, and told him about the two Hispanic men who arrived just before Danny at Cubano's.

"So, we have more people added to our suspect list." The

lieutenant couldn't hide the smile on his face when he said, "I assume we got some pictures of these other two guys."

I again, didn't want to throw Smitty under the bus, and the lieutenant wasn't expecting any photos anyway. "I don't think Smitty was close enough to get a good shot." I quickly moved on. "I told the shop steward for the union we would be back tomorrow, if that's OK with you. The picket line is directly across the street from Cubano's building and is a perfect location for seeing who comes and goes."

"Can you give a good description of these two guys?"

"Somewhat. Both looked to be Hispanic, late 20's or early 30's; one was wearing a black leather sport coat-looking jacket and jeans. The other guy was also dressed neatly. He was wearing a long, tan coat. I thought he was a bit overdressed, considering the warm weather."

"That's good, Rocco. I can tell you that I'm going to get shit from Smitty about going down there on a Saturday, I can't spare Andy for the day."

I didn't tell Capanno that Smitty had already made it clear that he would not be working on the weekend. "Lieu, if you have no problem with it, I can go down there by myself. I won't be doing anything more than walking on the picket line and keeping an eye on the building."

"OK, if you think you can handle it. I just don't want any cowboy getting his ass in a bind in the Bronx."

"I'll be fine. I want to write this report while I have descriptions of the two men fresh in my mind."

"OK, Rocco. Just do the surveillance detail then go home. No need to tie up an entire Saturday."

"I'll call you when I get back."

CHAPTER 35

Saturday, April 21st

Since I was going to the Bronx by myself, there was no reason to rush out of the house. I waited for my daughters to wake up and we enjoyed a lively family breakfast together. It was nice to spend some time with them, despite the banter that erupted.

"Hey, that's my brand-new sweater," Marie quipped. "Don't you have enough clothes of your own?"

Patrice snapped back. "You borrow mine!"

"Fine. Wear it," Marie reluctantly said, "but don't get it dirty."

Patrice smiled. "I promise, I won't. Thanks."

The drama was over and it was time to leave for work. I kissed Audrey and the girls goodbye. "See you ladies later."

I called Capanno before I left the house and told him I would check in with the desk officer to let him know where I was going.

"Good idea, Rocco. I want them to know where you are."

Sergeant Harrison was at the front desk when I arrived. I told him where I was going and what I would be doing. He laughed when I told him that the best spot for surveillance was on the picket line of hospital workers, right across the street from Cubano's building. I pulled the hat out of my pocket and put it on my head. Harrison laughed and called Officer Frank Johnson over to the desk.

"Hey Johnson, come and see this." Johnson had been with the department for twenty-two years. He mostly worked as the desk assistant in headquarters. The two officers laughed: the hat resembled the one that the ice-cream man wore while in his truck on his neighborhood route. Officer Johnson asked if I'd give him a Good Humor ice cream sandwich. It was definitely time to leave for the Bronx.

I parked the car on DeKalb Avenue, close to Gun Hill Road, in the event the same two individuals from Friday approached from that direction. If they did show up, I could walk toward the corner to see if they got into a vehicle. I checked before I went on to join the picketers; there were a couple of beat up vans and one car parked down the street. The car was an old blue Caprice without a front license plate. I chose not to check for the rear plate. I did not want to arouse suspicion.

I bought a couple of coffees at the deli on the corner and returned to the picket line. Ralph held up a thermos when I offered him one and said, "Thanks anyway, but I come prepared."

I gave the extra coffee to one of the other picketers.

"How's it going, Ralph?"

Looking at his skeleton crew on the picket line he said, "I'm happy I have the folks who did show up. How long are you planning to stay?"

"That depends on the activity across the street. Maybe, if our subject works, he'll be off on Saturdays so I'll get a glimpse."

There was not much foot traffic across the street, so anyone who did show would be obvious. Ralph and I walked and chatted for the better part of an hour. Then some activity broke out at the entrance to Cubano's building.

Two men came out of the front door, arguing loudly. They were so loud and rowdy that they drew the attention of the picketers, who stopped walking to watch the activity.

"Either of those two your suspect?" Ralph asked.

Neither was Cubano or Danny and neither looked like either of the Hispanic looking men I saw the other day. I shook my head, *no*.

The shouting continued, most of it in Spanish.

"Ralph, do you understand what they're saying?"

Ralph strained to hear as much of the shouting as possible. "Best I can figure is that the man with the blue T-shirt and brown shorts is accusing the other guy of screwing his wife or girlfriend, or both."

From seemingly out of nowhere, a machete appeared and the fight escalated. "Estás muerto pedazo de mierda!"

Ralph leaned in toward me and translated, "He's calling him a piece of shit..."

I stopped Ralph mid-sentence. "I know enough Spanish to recognize the other words as *you're dead*. Where the fuck did that machete come from?"

"Beats the shit out of me, but he sure seems intent on using it." Looks like our hospital ER may be getting some business."

Even though I was out of my jurisdiction, I was still a police officer and had a duty to prevent a crime, especially a murder.

"Shit," I thought, this is going to blow my cover and it sure as hell is not going to make Lieutenant Capanno happy. I could still hear his words; *I don't want any cowboy getting his ass in a bind in the Bronx.*

Thankfully, an NYPD squad car pulled up and two officers jumped out. I was impressed by how quickly they brought the situation under control. Within seconds, the machete-wielding man was in cuffs and put in a squad car. Two additional cars arrived and the younger man was taken in handcuffs by the officers to one of them. The police left and the picketers went back to their line.

"That sure broke the monotony," Ralph smiled and he, too, resumed the picketing as though nothing out of the ordinary had happened.

Things had just settled down when I saw Danny's car pull up. He double- parked close to the building. Either he did not intend to be inside very long, or he assumed that parking restrictions were not enforced on the weekend. He was in the apartment for about 45 minutes. When he came out, he was alone.

I waited another hour or two to see if anyone else might show up, but there was no more activity around Cubano's alley. It was time to call it a day.

I said goodbye to Ralph, thanked him for his help. When I got back to my car, I radioed the desk sergeant to let him know I was heading back to headquarters. The blue Caprice was still there but there were too many people around for me to examine a rear plate. "Anything you guys want me to pick up on my way in?"

"If it's not too much trouble Rocco, could you stop at Geno's Deli and get two coffees with milk and sugar and two buttered rolls?"

"No problem, Sarge." I was a bit hungry myself so the excuse to stop at Geno's Deli in Lakeside was welcomed.

Sergeant Harrison was happy to see me when I returned. "How'd you make out down there, Rocco?"

"I would say the trip was worth it. One of our suspects returned."

Harrison took a sip of his coffee. "Why is that good?"

"That's twice in two days. He's a frequent visitor, and my guess is that he's involved with the building super in the murders. I'm going to call Lieutenant Capanno to let him know I'm back."

I stayed to write my report of the day's surveillance. It was half-past three before I was ready to head home. I waved goodbye to Harrison, "See you on Monday, Sarge. I hope the rest of today and Sunday stays quiet for you."

"OK Rocco, you enjoy, too. I'll sign you out for today."

Officer Johnson, who had been working all day, called out

from his side of the desk, "When you come in next week, I'll have a vanilla cone."

I laughed good naturedly as I walk out the door. "Not funny, Frank."

CHAPTER 36

Monday, April 23rd

Capanno was reading my report when I got to headquarters on Monday afternoon.

"You know, Lieu, this guy Danny makes regular trips to Cubano's apartment, even though he claims he doesn't know the super all that well. He's not very bright and he seems scared of something or someone."

"What do you think we can do to put pressure on him, Rocco?"

"I think we ought to pay him another visit, put his feet to the fire and accuse him of being involved in the murders."

Capanno rubbed his chin. "Do you think that would push him to run? It doesn't sound to me as if he has a whole lot keeping him glued to this area."

"I don't think he would make a move without his father, his father isn't going to leave that club. After we talk to him, we'll keep a close eye on him to see where he goes and what he does. If he doesn't see or hear from us for a while, he'll figure we really don't have anything on him and he'll get careless."

"Sounds good. I'll run it by the ADA to see what he thinks. Meanwhile, I've got another burglary to give you. There are some things about this one that are similar to our unsolved burglary. Seems our thief may have left some evidence this time. Patrol secured the scene and the homeowner is waiting for your arrival."

"Got it Lieu. Where's the house?"

"57 Sunnyvale Avenue, first floor apartment, which happens to be right around the corner from the other open burglary. It's the home of a Mr. and Mrs. Stevens and their daughter."

"I'll go right over. Let me know what the ADA says about the homicide case."

"I'll be out of here when you get back. Give me a call at home to let me know how you make out with the burglary. By then, I'll be able to fill you in on whatever the ADA says."

I headed out to speak with the homeowners. Mr. John Stevens met me at the door. I introduced myself and showed him my identification.

He was clearly shaken and quickly assured me that no one had touched anything in the apartment after he discovered it was broken into.

"What time did you notice the break-in, Sir?"

"About an hour ago, about 3PM, we were away for a couple of days. I saw that a jar in which we kept some cash had been knocked off the fireplace mantle; the money was gone. I went upstairs to the woman on the second floor to call the police, I don't know the guy who lives in the third-floor apartment, so I sent my wife and daughter to stay at my sister-in-law's house until things were settled. The first officer to arrive determined that the thief was not in the apartment and allowed me to come back inside."

Officer Tom O'Malley had been waiting to speak to me. "When I got here, I checked the apartment to make sure it was secure. Then I asked Mr. Stevens to tell me exactly what he did once he noticed things were out of place. He told me what he repeated for you. I instructed Mr. Stevens to wait with me in the lobby until you arrived."

"Thanks, Tom. I'm hoping that whoever hit this place left some evidence and that we can connect him or her to the other burglary I have around the corner. Hitting an apartment in a multi-family house wouldn't really fit the M.O., but who knows."

Officer O'Malley, Mr. Stevens, and I walked through the apartment to identify anything else that may have been disturbed. When we got to the master bedroom, Mr. Stevens indicated that several dresser drawers were open and the clothes rifled through. One drawer had, in fact, contained some expensive jewelry. The jewelry, like the money, was gone.

The rest of the apartment was intact.

Back in the living room, I asked, "Mr. Stevens, do you use a cleaning service?"

"Yes, we use a service. Usually the same woman once every two weeks; sometimes she brings someone with her to help but she's not due until next week."

"We'll need the name of the service and the workers' names. I'm also going to leave a property deposition form on which you can list the stolen items. With your permission, I'll take that jar for processing. I'm sure it's safe for your wife and daughter to come home.

"Anything else, Tom?"

"No, Rocco. That's about it. I checked with the woman upstairs, Mrs. Wilson, but she says she didn't hear or see anything. No one was home in the third-floor apartment."

As soon as I got back to headquarters, I saw a note on my desk from the lieutenant advising me to give him a call.

"Hello, Lieu, I got your note."

"How did the burglary investigation go?"

"I brought a piece of evidence back to process; I'm just getting ready to dust it for prints. What did the ADA say?"

"He said we can give one more shot to the Varanda kid, but we cannot reveal any evidence we have. Just throw a scare into him, see what kind of response we get."

"Detective Smith and I can go down next week."

"Smitty is out again with his bad back. You can go with Andy when one of your shifts overlap."

"Thanks, Lieu. I'll keep you up to speed on this burglary."

I dusted the jar and got lucky. I was able to get some clear prints.

I called Mr. Stevens. "Mr. Stevens, this is Officer DeMarco."

Mr. Stevens was still shaken. "Yes Officer, I have those property sheets made out. I also have some photos of some of the jewelry that is missing."

"You do?"

"Yes. Our insurance agent advised us to take pictures when we bought some of the pieces in case we ever had to file a claim."

"Smart." I said. "I called to ask if we could fingerprint you, your wife and your daughter to eliminate your prints from several prints we got off the jar."

"Of course."

"Thank you. I will contact you if we have need for anything else."

I lifted some prints from the jar to check against recent prints that we had on file. It was a shot in the dark, but cases have been solved with less. At this point, it would take a little luck to go with investigative skills.

The rest of my tour was quiet. By the time I headed home it was midnight.

CHAPTER 37

Monday, April 30th

After spending the better part of a week examining prints and checking pawn shop sheets for my open burglary investigations, I wasn't any closer to closing either one. I remembered what Roberts said when he asked me, *"what do you think your chances are for solving them?"* I put the burglaries on the back burner until new leads on them developed.

I returned my focus back to the homicide case. Lieutenant Capanno walked by my desk holding a cup of coffee. "How'd you make out with the prints and pawn sheets, Rocco?"

"No closer than I was Lieu."

"Don't let it get you down Kid. Burglaries are a bitch to solve. Andy's coming in Wednesday. Get back to your plan with the homicide."

"Great," I said. "We can make our Bronx run. I think we should confront Danny without his father present."

Wednesday, May 2nd
As soon as Scollari came in, we confirmed the plan to return to the Bronx. The Lieutenant brought Andy up-to-date on the details.

"We got time to get coffee before we go down, Kid?"

"Absolutely!"

During our trip to the Bronx we shared stories about our kids. Andy warned me as to what I should be prepared for as they got older. We joked about some of the things that had gone on at the office; it was a comfortable partnership.

We parked on a side street near the club. As we got out of the car, Andy pointed. "Isn't that Danny's car over there, Kid?"

"Good observation, *Old Man*. There's nothing that gets by you."

We laughed and Andy knocked on the door.

The Varanda boy looked through the peek hole, saw us, and sighed, "Now what?"

"Danny, come outside. We want to ask you a couple of questions and we'd like to take you for a short drive. Can you leave the club for a little while?"

"Yeah, my dad will be here later, though."

This made things a little easier. We didn't have to explain to the father why we were taking his son for a drive and Danny came willingly.

"I'll drive, Rocco. We'll take the scenic route."

Once we got in the car, Danny said, "What scenic route?" His eyes darted back and forth between Andy and me. "Where are we going? To your police station?"

Danny Varanda was beginning to squirm.

"No, you aren't under arrest. We want to ask you some questions away from your club. Trust me, we aren't leaving the Bronx."

Andy and I took turns asking him questions he had already answered to see if we could trip him up.

"Tell me again, when was the last time you saw those girls?" I asked.

"How often are you at Cubano's?" Andy asked without giving him a chance to think about either question.

His face showed concern when we asked the question about Cubano's apartment.

"I told you guys already. I hardly ever go there. The last time I was there was when I brought you guys."

I nodded. "And the only other time before that was when you brought the girls, right?"

"Yeah, I think," Danny said, "but I don't remember when that was."

"Was it weeks ago? Months ago?" Andy asked.

"Wait, you're confusing me. I took the girls right before they were supposed to have the party. And that was a while ago."

I looked at him coldly. "And your last visit to Cubano's?"

"When I took you guys."

"Okay," I said. "And you haven't been there since?"

He shook his head and whispered, "Yup."

As clueless as Danny was, he recognized the route we were taking was to Cubano's neighborhood. "We're not going to Cubano's again, are we?"

I turned to look at him. "Would you have a problem with that, Danny?"

"No, I just don't know what more you want to ask him and why you want me with you when you talk to him."

I rubbed my chin and smiled. "Are you afraid we may ask you questions in front of him that would make Cubano nervous? Are you worried about how you would answer them?"

The closer we got closer to Cubano's place; the more nervous Danny became.

"Danny, you said you hardly ever go to this guy's house. You know what I think?" I asked.

Danny shook his head.

"I think that's a crock of shit! You know it and we know it. I'm not sure why you make so many visits to Cubano's place, but we are getting more than a little suspicious about your and Cubano's involvement in these murders."

Danny held out his hands, pleading, "You got it all wrong. I only go there to get drugs to sell. Small amounts so I can make some money."

"So," I said, "small drug sales. That's how you make your money?"

"Kind of. My father gives me some money for gas and shit, but not much. Are you going to turn me in on the drug shit?"

I shook my head. "We told you before and we'll tell you again, we don't care about your bullshit drug dealings or your father's illegal club. That's the NYPD's problem. We're only interested in the murder of the two young girls. Girls who you admitted to bringing to Cubano's place. Then you claim you haven't seen since." We pulled up right in front of Cubano's apartment building, double-parked and let the engine idle.

"That's true, I did bring them and I haven't seen them since."

I glared at him. "Could that be because they never left here alive?"

"They were alive when I left."

"Now, why don't we believe that?" I looked over at Andy who, I could tell, was chuckling silently. He knew we had this kid shitting in his pants. "So, what should we do Andy, lock this little prick up? Or, go inside and tell Cubano that Danny ratted him out?"

Danny was pale and his lips trembled. We decided to let him digest our conversation before heading back to his dad's club.

Danny kept saying, "I didn't have anything to do with those girls getting killed. Let's just get outta here, OK?"

By the time Andy pulled out into traffic, we thought the kid was going to start crying.

"Am I free to go?" he asked, almost pleading, when we arrived back at the club.

"Did you kill those girls, Danny?" I asked.

"No, I didn't. I swear!"

"Well if you were there when they were killed, you are just as guilty." I looked over at Andy who nodded in agreement. "We don't have enough to charge you right now, but you can count on this. The next time you see *me*, I will be putting cuffs on you for murder. Do you understand?"

"Yes, I promise, I didn't kill them!"

"OK, Get out."

Danny couldn't get out of the car fast enough. We headed for the Bronx River Parkway.

Andy smiled. "We owe ourselves a Smitty-style breakfast before we get back to headquarters."

"I definitely agree!"

"I think our suspicions are spot-on. That little prick either participated in the killings or, at the very least, was there. He kept whining, *I didn't kill those girls*, but not once did he say, *We didn't kill those girls*. Let's see how the ADA wants to proceed, I think we found our weak link, Kid."

"I couldn't agree with you more, Old Man." We enjoyed our breakfast and headed back to Lakeside.

CHAPTER 38

Sergeant Winston was at the front desk when we arrived back at headquarters. Without a glance up from the newspaper, he said, "Capanno told me to tell you guys that he went to the DA's office and that he'll call you."

"Thanks, Sarge. Did he say when?"

"I don't know. Just wait for him to call."

"Hang in there, Rocco," Andy said, smiling when he saw me shaking my head at Winston's apathy. "Winston will be retiring soon; your promotion will be coming up and you're on your way to solving a big homicide."

He made me smile. "I think our drive with Danny went well. That dumb-ass kid knows what happened."

The phone rang.

"You pick it up, Kid. I'm sure it's about the case."

"DeMarco, Lakeside Detective Division." It was the lieutenant.

Andy and I just got back, Lieu. We were talking about how that kid, Danny, looked like he was ready to shit in his pants this morning."

I heard Capanno exhale cigarette smoke. "I'm at the DA's office. ADA Bishop is anxious to hear the status of the investigation, including this morning's interview."

Assistant District Attorney John Bishop was a well-respected member of the District Attorney's office. At 35, he was no longer fresh out of law school. Bishop presented a commanding presence in the courtroom – he stood 6'3". He had been in the District Attorney's Homicide Division for five years.

"Things went well, Lieu. We put a real scare into Danny Varanda. Andy and I agree that he is the weakest link in what is becoming a chain of suspects. We made it clear that we strongly suspect him of being involved in these murders." I filled the lieutenant in on the specifics of our conversation with Danny.

"Good. I'm sure Bishop will want to talk with you. We'll call you back after I let him know about Varanda."

"Why was the call so brief?" Andy asked.

"He's going to bring the ADA up to speed and call right back. I'm curious to hear what Bishop thinks we should do next. He has to make sure we have a case he can prosecute."

It didn't take long before the lieutenant called back. "OK, Rocco, I talked to Bishop. He thinks we should back off the suspects for now. He wants us to get usable information for a prosecution. He doesn't want us to keep going down there and pumping the suspects if we can't make any arrests. If we stay away, they may get confident thinking that they have pulled this off and get sloppy, maybe give us something to hang on them."

"Does he have a problem with what we did with Danny this morning?"

"No. Bishop agrees with your assessment, Danny is the weak link. He wants us to try to set something up, get him to turn on the others."

"Lay off the kid *and* set something up? How does he suggest we do that?"

"Hold on a minute." I could hear Capanno talking with ADA Bishop. He came back on the line. "I'm putting you on speaker. What do you guys think Danny has that we can lean on and then use?"

"He admitted that he goes to this guy Cubano to get drugs to sell. He says it's small scale stuff, but I don't believe the majority of what this moron says."

Bishop spoke up, "We can take advantage of Danny's drug

activity. Work him for a while and set him up for one big score. Maybe he'll make a deal on drug charges and turn on this Cubano."

Capanno picked up the conversation, "Bishop has two officers he believes can be helpful. They've done things like this before and know how to take advantage of any weaknesses young Mr. Danny Varanda may have."

Bishop continued, "My people can work this kid on his need for money and his need to show his father he's not a useless moron. You guys said the kid is infatuated with women?"

"Seems like he is," I said. "Although the women we spoke to think he's an idiot."

"Bishop's two undercover detectives, Matteo Garcia and Teresa Lopez, are familiar with the Bronx. They have not gone after marks down there, so there is no chance they'll be recognized."

"How are they going to connect with Danny?"

"We'll give them information on the club. They have ways of working their way in. Just an FYI, they take time doing their thing to lessen suspicion. We're going to have to be patient."

I figured that comment was a shot at me. Patience is not exactly my strong suit. "Sounds good, Lieu. Tell them to contact me or Andy if they need any background information."

"They are going to meet us at headquarters," Capanno said. "We'll give them everything we've got and they'll run their plan by us; we'll make sure things make sense."

CHAPTER 39

After a week of 4 − 12 shifts and a couple of days off, I was back in for the day shifts on Tuesday, May 15th.

I had been working on a number of different local cases. I had a report of a stolen car, which turned out to be a case of unauthorized use by the complainant's son; and vandalism to the greens on the golf course of our northern most country club. The primary suspect in the golf course vandalism was believed to be 15 years old, so the case was turned over to our youth division.

I was waiting to hear from Bishop's detectives. Finally, about 10:30AM, the call came in. "Good morning. Officer DeMarco? This is Matteo Garcia."

"How are you? Please call me Rocco."

"I'm good, thanks. Would today be a good day for me and Teresa to meet with you at your headquarters?"

"Today would be great," I said. "Detective Andy Scollari is here, too. What time do you want to meet?"

"How about in an hour?"

"That's fine. We'll see you soon." I hurried in to Lieutenant Capanno's office to ask if he could meet with us as well.

"I'm interested in meeting them. You and Andy can handle the conversation."

Detectives Garcia and Lopez arrived promptly at 11:45AM. "Can I get you some coffee?" I showed them into Capanno's office, where we could talk comfortably and privately.

"No thanks, were OK on coffee."

Detective Matteo Garcia was thirty-two years old, an

imposing, solid, athletic figure. Teresa Lopez was an interesting complement: 28, almost as tall as Garcia's 6 feet, but slender as the proverbial rail.

"How long have you been on undercover drug investigations?" I asked.

"I've been in the undercover aspect for about 4 years," Garcia answered. "Teresa, about 3 years."

I nodded. "Do you always work together?"

"Not all the time. It depends on the case and the target of the investigation. We think our cover will work well this time."

I didn't imagine many drug dealers expected to meet *couples* as undercover cops.

"After we establish initial rapport with this Varanda," Garcia said, "We'll allow a good period of time between transactions. This way we won't raise suspicion."

"We know you guys want this case to move, but these drug deals can take time." Teresa added. "We promise that we will keep you informed as to how we are doing."

"Give us the details about the club this kid's father owns," Garcia said.

"It's a low-end hole in the wall that seems to be a hangout for most of the neighborhood skells and skanks," Andy volunteered. "I think if Danny is doing drug deals there, it's small-time stuff. He's likely selling when his father isn't around; his dad gave us the impression that he thinks Danny has nothing to do with drugs. If he is dealing big, I doubt it's in the club."

"It seems to me that Danny spends more time in the club than his dad does," I said. "Seems his dad travels frequently. So *maybe* some bigger deals do go down there." The visiting detectives nodded. "Danny makes frequent visits to a guy called *Cubano* on DeKalb; he claims that's where he buys the drugs that he sells."

"We'll frequent the club a few times...have some drinks, chat with some of the regulars," Garcia explained. "Eventually, when Danny gets used to seeing us, we'll connect with him. If he's doing things with other people, it works well. It takes the focus off of him and he'll be less suspicious. We'll start with small buys every now and then to earn his trust. We will assess his capability of making a big score. Even if he's working for someone else and is only going to get a cut, he may be willing to sell."

"Sounds to us like your other suspect, the super, is his main supplier." Teresa added, "This Cuban may be a hardcore criminal; he hasn't survived this long by being stupid. If he thinks there might be some big money to be made, he'll use someone else to do the deal. This way, if something goes down, he's not the one holding the dope, literally. Do you think this kid will roll on him?"

"I'm sure he would do almost anything to keep himself out of trouble. But I believe he is terrified of this Cubano; he might not roll too easily if he believes Cubano will kill him. And Danny does believe that Cubano wouldn't hesitate to kill him," I said confidently. "I've seen the *enforcer* tattoo on Cubano's hand, so we know he's been a murderer in Cuba. I doubt he has problems killing here. Please be careful."

Garcia nodded at Teresa. "Thanks for the warning. As Teresa said, it will take time. But from what I'm hearing, this is something we can pull off. We'll be in contact with ADA Bishop and Lieutenant Capanno, and we'll keep you guys in the loop."

Capanno, who had been listening intently, nodded in agreement. "We're looking forward to the break we need to solve this case. Good luck."

Andy and I watched the two detectives leave. It would be several weeks before anything happened.

CHAPTER 40

Tuesday June, 19th

We had finally gotten word that detectives Garcia and Lopez were ready to make a large buy, which would result in a serious felony charge against Danny. We didn't know exactly when, but Lieutenant Capanno would let us know.

My rotation in the Detective Bureau ended, so I was back in uniform around the clock in the patrol division. I was told that my promotion to sergeant was imminent.

Finally, on Tuesday, June 19th, a month after the meeting with the County detectives, I got the call I had been waiting for. The buy was going down in Yonkers. Before Lieutenant Capanno finished telling me to get to headquarters ASAP, I was already on my way. Capanno was pulling me back out of patrol into the detective unit to continue working this double homicide.

Andy was ready to go and waiting in the car when I arrived. "I'll drive," he said. "The lieutenant told me exactly where we were going."

My eyes darted around the bureau. "Where's Detective Smith?"

"Still in bed with his bad back."

We parked our unmarked car a few blocks from where the deal was to take place. There were back-up units in the area from both the Westchester County Police and Yonkers police departments.

At 3:30 PM, we got a radio call that the buy had been made and the suspect was in custody. We were told to come to the location of the bust, only two blocks from where we were waiting.

Danny, already handcuffed, was put in the rear seat of our car. He, along with three other people, had agreed to sell Garcia and Lopez 10 oz. of cocaine, with a street value of about thirty-five thousand dollars. The Yonkers police took the other three suspects into custody.

When he saw me, what had been fright turned to sheer panic. His eyes widened and he began to hyperventilate.

"I told you the next time you saw me, I'd be arresting you for murder, didn't I, Danny?"

"But this was a drug thing. Right?"

"Yes, a drug thing, for which you can go to jail for a very long time. I want you to think about that while we drive to headquarters."

"Where are you taking me?"

"Our house, Lakeside Police Department."

We brought Danny in the back door. We put him in the small, brightly lit, interview room. A uniformed officer stayed with him. The presence of the officer was intended to remind him of how much trouble he was in.

Outside the interview room ADA Bishop, Lieutenant Capanno, me, Andy, and two additional District Attorney investigators, Jack O'Marra and James Sanflone were gathered.

Danny was read his rights for the second time that evening and made to understand the gravity of his situation by ADA Bishop. "You know you are here on an A-1 felony, which could send you to prison for at least twenty years. Do you understand that? Do you want a lawyer?"

"How does my drug bust connect me with a murder case?" Danny's voice was shaky.

Bishop shook his head. "You didn't answer my questions. Do you understand your rights? Do you want a lawyer?"

"No, I mean yes, I understand. I don't want a lawyer. I just want to know what's happening."

"We know you were involved in the murders of Lola Vasquez and Crystal Ramos, Danny. We don't know yet know the full extent of your involvement, though. How much you tell us may have a significant impact on your future."

"I didn't kill those girls. I told *them*." Danny pointed at me and Andy.

Bishop pointed at Danny. "Then it must have been your father. Did *he* kill them?"

"He didn't either. We were there, so I can tell you what happened, but me and my father didn't kill anyone." Danny had again spoken impulsively and had, in his panic, said too much.

"OK, Danny," Bishop said as he folded his hands and leaned in toward Danny. "Here's what we'll do. If the information you give us is correct – and you are willing to testify to it – we can make the drug charge go away." Reading a look of confusion on Danny's face, Bishop said, "Do you know what immunity means?"

Danny looked up at Bishop. "Can you do that?"

Bishop leaned back. "Yeah, I can do that. You do realize that by being there and witnessing the murders, you can be charged as an accessory and can be charged with the same crimes. We may be able to work with you on that. But you have to talk. Now."

Danny looked as though he might puke. "OK, me and my father were there, but Cubano threatened us. He said that if we said anything, he would kill us."

"We can give you protection until the trial if that's what you are worried about."

"Well, yeah, I am worried about that. Cubano told us, do as I say or you are both dead."

"OK Danny, we need to know exactly what Cubano did and what he ordered you and your father to do. We are going to record your statement on videotape.-Don't leave anything out, even if it makes you feel bad or responsible. Do you understand?"

Danny was on the verge of tears. "Yes, Yes, I understand."

ADA Bishop asked me to stay in the room during Danny's statement to see if it coincided with information we already had.

Bishop spoke without emotion. After preliminary questions to establish Danny's full name and address and his full understanding of the circumstances, Bishop intensified the interrogation. "Danny, did there come a time on February 4th of this year that you brought two girls, Lola Vasquez and Crystal Ramos, to an apartment on DeKalb Avenue to purchase drugs for a party they were going to have?"

"I don't know the date exactly, but I do know it was the beginning of February. On a Saturday."

"Tell us what happened when you got there."

Danny proceeded to describe the details of the murders at Cubano's apartment. He said, "Cubano appeared to be more high than usual and there were two other guys there."

"Who were the other guys?" Bishop pressed.

"We only know them by nicknames, *Tramposo* and *Vato*. Both of those guys and Cubano had guns. Cubano made sure we knew he would kill me and my father."

"Keep going, Danny."

"Cubano got pissed off when he took a look at a little notebook Lola always carried. He saw the letters "P" and "D" and thought that meant she was a cop. Lola insisted she wasn't, but he decided to kill the girls. Really, just like that. He just decided to kill them. After tying them up, Cubano strangled both girls and had Vato and Tramposo them put in trash bags. While we waited to see what he was going to do next, he snorted some more coke. He decided we were going to dump the bodies somewhere; he put one in my trunk and the other in the trunk of a car belonging to Vato or Tramposo. I'm not sure whose car it was, but it looked like an old beat up police car."

I didn't interrupt but thought about the car matching that description that was parked on DeKalb during my surveillance.

Danny continued. "He split up me and my father. Tramposo got into my car with me. He told me to follow Vato. Cubano put my father in the other car with him and Vato. It was dark and I had to follow that other car. We pulled into City Island, but when we were going to dump the bodies, Cubano saw headlights coming toward us and he said to find a different place."

"Who did the headlights belong to?"

"It was a fucking city bus. So, we left and we wound up on the Hutchinson River Parkway. Cubano figured bodies dumped upstate would not be connected to the Bronx. It started to snow and the streets were getting slippery. He didn't want us to get stuck with bodies in the cars. He had us pull off the parkway and drive up a hill. We started to skid so he said to pull to the side of the road and dump the bags."

"Wasn't he afraid of someone seeing you?"

"When we were out of the cars and lifting the bags from the trunks, Vato asked Cubano what to do if someone stopped and saw us. Cubano said *shoot them*. Vato said, 'Suppose it's a cop?' Cubano said, 'Especially if it's a cop. Fuckin shoot him.' Cubano did not like cops."

Danny continued with the story relating the trip back to the Bronx. When he finished, Bishop, the lieutenant, and I stepped outside the room.

Bishop turned to me. "Officer DeMarco, is his story consistent with evidence you have?"

"Yes. Things he said made sense, based on our evidence."

"The best way to confirm his story is to go get the father and question him separately. See how close the stories are."

I agreed.

Lieutenant Capanno nodded. "Go get the father."

Andy and I, along with Bishop's investigators, used a van belonging to the DA's office and drove back to the Bronx.

By the time we pulled up in front of the club, it was late, a little after 10:00PM. The two investigators went into the club while Andy and I waited in the van.

Andy became anxious. "This is taking too long. I feel like we're a target just sitting here."

"Relax. I have my gun aimed at the window. If someone tries to do anything to us, I'll shoot them."

"Shit," he said. "That's all we need."

The investigators came out with Mr. Varanda and put him in the back third tier of the van. He had the same looks of shock and fear that his son had when he saw me and Andy show up at the drug bust.

When we got to headquarters, Mr. Varanda was interrogated with the same questions that his son had been asked, by Bishop, on videotape. His version of the of the murders was close enough to Danny's to allow corroboration. We knew they were telling the truth.

Bishop explained Danny's situation to Mr. Varanda, emphasizing the need for court testimony to avoid serious drug charges and possibly, murder charges. Bishop coldly advised him of the ramifications if either refused. "You know how much trouble your son is in already without the murder charges, right?"

He looked down at the floor. Reluctantly, he said, "I'll do whatever is needed." He shook his head. "Sí, I know how much trouble that imbécil is in."

Mr. Varanda knew what Cubano would do to him and to his son if the Cuban killer didn't wind up in jail.

Out of earshot of the two men, Bishop said, "You do realize this is going to put a price on their heads."

I looked at the lieutenant. "I don't give a shit. Do you, Lieu?"

"No, I don't care. Fuck them. They were just as involved; we're using them because without their testimony, it would be a hard case to prove."

CHAPTER 41

At half-past midnight, Wednesday, June 20th, Bishop obtained an arrest warrant for Cubano. The warrant was considered a "No Knock" warrant: forcible entry was permissible and the subject need not be alerted to the entry.

"It'll be me, you, Detective Burns, investigators O'Marra and Sanflone, and, from what I understand, two more of Bishop's investigators. Bishop and I agree that we should try to push through the night, not waste any time. We'll go to the NYPD 50th Precinct and meet up with a Lieutenant Johnson, who runs the Emergency Services Unit (ESU) there. Knowing NYPD, we'll have plenty of support. They don't hold back."

"What about Andy?"

"Andy asked to not be part of this. He's had enough, as he said, of those scumbags."

Capanno paused and sat back in his chair. "Rocco, this could get hairy. We know there are guns and this Cubano is a dope-snorting head case. He's already killed two people. We know he doesn't like cops. Make sure you have your body armor."

"Don't worry, Lieu."

"I want you and Barney to take shotguns as well. We don't know if these other two guys, Tramposo and Vato, will be there."

At 2:30AM, we headed to the 50th Precinct. When we walked inside, it was obvious that the desk sergeant was expecting us.

"The lieutenant is waiting for you," he said, pointing toward the stairwell. "Upstairs, third door on the right."

The 50th looked a lot like other precincts I had been in. The building seemed to be a hundred years old; updating was not in a police department's budget.

The lieutenant's office was the bright spot of the precinct building. There were plaques and commendations on the painted walls; his large, wooden desk looked as if it could be in a CEO's office. There were pictures of his family on the wide surface of the desk; judging by the approximate ages of his children, I guessed that he had to be in his early to mid-fifties. Johnson was in excellent shape. He set a good example for his subordinates.

"Why don't you go down the hall," Johnson said to our group of officers, pointing to the right with his thumb. "Go into the break room. We have coffee and donuts in there. I'm sure you could all use some caffeine." He shifted his attention to Lieutenant Capanno, who was standing in front of the desk. "What good police station would be without coffee and do-nuts, right? I'll have some brought in here for us." He held his hand out, formally introduced himself to Lieutenant Capanno and said, "Let me see the warrant."

I turned to follow the others when Lieutenant Capanno invited me to stay. He introduced me to Johnson and then handed the warrant over.

"These no-knocks can get hairy," Johnson said, perusing the page. "The warrant lists this one individual but we have no way of knowing how many people will be in there."

Capanno nodded. "No, we don't."

"DeKalb Avenue huh? Not really the worst part of the Bronx. What are we looking at here in the way of suspects and fire power?"

Taking an offered seat, Capanno said, "Based on our intel, Lieutenant Johnson..."

Johnson interrupted with a smile and offered me a seat as well. "Call me Frank."

"OK Frank, thanks. We could be looking at three or more

armed individuals who, by all accounts, are not the least bit hesitant to resist with force."

Thankfully, an officer knocked and entered with mugs of hot coffee. I had a fleeting yearning for Mrs. Ramos' caffeine-spiked brew to keep me wide-eyed through the rest of the night and the early hours of the coming day.

"Call me Randy," Capanno returned Frank Johnson's in-formality. "This is Officer Rocco DeMarco. He's the lead in-vestigator on the case. Got put in the bureau on a Monday and drew this double homicide that Thursday."

Johnson laughed. "Quite a way to start off as a detective, Rocco."

"I'm not a detective, sir. I'm supposed to be promoted to sergeant soon."

Johnson said with a smile, "After this case, whatever the position, you'll be well-prepared. Let's go down the hall to fin-ish our coffee before the donuts are all gone. Then we'll head out."

When we entered the break room, I was taken aback by the crowd. In addition to our people, there were at least another fifteen uniformed officers of the Emergency Services Unit. They were in full SWAT gear.

It was now 4AM.

"Randy," Johnson said, "is there anyone in your group who knows this guy? Someone who has been there before?"

I didn't give Lieutenant Capanno a chance to answer, I spoke up like a kid in school, eager to answer a teacher's ques-tion. "I'm the only one who Cubano knows. I questioned him about his knowledge of the two girls and his criminal history in Cuba. I'm sure he'd recognize me."

"Why don't we do this? Instead of busting in there and risking a firefight, why don't we have Officer DeMarco knock on his door?" He turned to Capanno. "Cubano has seen your officer before and he won't feel as threatened or possibly go off if he sees one officer. Who knows what this bastard will do if a half-dozen armed cops storm his apartment. The rest of us will stay out of the line of sight until he opens the door."

Capanno turned to me. "What do you think, Rocco? You willing to do that?"

"Of course. I'm sure it will be fine, Lieu." Turning back to Lieutenant Johnson, I asked, "What do I do when he answers the door?"

"When he opens the door, just step out of the way and we'll be on him like flies on shit. He'll be on the floor in cuffs before he has any time to react."

"We'll launch at 8AM," Johnson said.

Capanno put his arm around my shoulder and smiled. "I'm sure Smitty would insist that you go in first, too." We both laughed, easing the tension for a minute or two.

The men began to organize and head out to their cars and vans; each was wearing a helmet, body-armor vest, and carried automatic rifles. As I zipped my windbreaker over my bullet-proof vest, I looked at the lieutenant and nodded that I was ready.

All of us – city and suburb cops alike – wanted to bring down Cubano.

CHAPTER 42

Wednesday, June 20th

O ur caravan resembled a military convoy. I was afraid that the presence of so many police vehicles would negate our efforts to surprise Cubano. I took my concern to Lieutenant Johnson. "Hey Lieu, what's this guy gonna think when he sees all the police vehicles on his street?"

"Not to worry, Rocco, there will only be one or two vehicles on his block until entry has been made." Then he smiled confidently. "Once we're in, the ESU response team will pull up to our location. No one will screw with us."

We arrived shortly after 8, high on caffeine and adrenaline.

I walked quickly down the alley to the basement entrance of Cubano's building. "Breathe," I said to myself.

ESU officers walked stealthily behind me. We stopped briefly outside the basement door. One of the officers whispered, "Describe this basement as best you can. Tell me about the location of the suspect's apartment door."

"The basement's open, but dark. The apartment door is about twenty-five feet in a straight line across from the basement entrance."

"Any obstacles in that space? Stuff like tools or appliances or shit like that?"

"There was nothing like that in the middle of the floor the last time I was here. It doesn't appear as though this super does much other than dump trash."

Another officer quietly said, "And bodies."

"We'll stay close," the ESU officer on point whispered. "We'll be out of site, right behind you, until our suspect opens the door. When that door opens, get the hell out of the way."

He didn't have to tell me that twice. I looked over the armed squad of men behind me and I was glad to oblige. I kept my own shotgun in easy reach, hidden behind my leg.

I approached the door with a sense of calm and confidence, which came as a welcomed surprise.

I knocked sharply on the apartment door with my left hand. As soon as I knocked, the unlocked door slowly swung open into the apartment. I did as I had been told and stepped out of the way, right away.

Four heavily armed ESU officers blew into the apartment. There was a young man sleeping on a bed that had been pushed against the side of the room. He bolted upright and faced a line of automatic rifles aimed directly and purposely at his head.

No one else was in the apartment.

"Officer DeMarco, do you know this guy?"

"I've never seen him before," I answered.

"No mas!" the man stammered.

"He's not Cubano and he looks nothing like either of the two guys I saw go into the apartment during my surveillance. He doesn't match the description the Varanda kid gave us of Vato or Tramposo."

The young man only spoke Spanish. He could barely stop shaking long enough to communicate with the four Kevlar-clad officers who were still pointing guns at him. He said something about coming to the apartment once in a while to sleep.

An ESU officer who spoke Spanish asked him "¿Dónde está Cubano?"

"No sé," he answered, trembling.

The officer turned to me and said, "I believe he doesn't

know, but we'll take him in for questioning. Cubano has to be around here somewhere. The door was open."

We quickly moved outside. I looked up and down the street, which was lined with ESU vehicles and NYPD patrol cars. When I looked toward Gun Hill Road, I couldn't believe my eyes.

Walking down the street in black flip-flops, a filthy, ill-fitting T-shirt and dirty, tan pants, was Cubano. He had the morning newspaper tucked under his arm and a coffee cup in his hands, oblivious to the police activity around him.

"There he is!" I pointed and said in disbelief.

In an instant, Cubano was face-to-face with two armed officers. "Get down, flat on your stomach, arms out from your sides!" one officer shouted at him.

"What the fuck!" Cubano blurted.

More officers closed in on him.

"Get down on your fat gut!" I shouted.

As he complied, his coffee cup flew out of his hand and coffee spilled across the sidewalk and into the street.

"Keep your fucking hands out to your side!" another officer shouted. He grabbed Cubano's left arm, put his knee into Cubano's shoulder, and quickly cuffed and searched the killer. Cubano glared up at me.

I smiled down at him. "Remember me, *amigo*?"

"Fuck you," was the best Cubano could do.

I read him his rights, carefully enunciating each word. "Do you understand these rights?" I asked him, loud enough to ensure that the other officers heard his response.

"Sí."

"In English!"

"Yes, I understand, pig." Cubano all but spit the words in my direction.

Lieutenant Capanno put his hand on my shoulder. "I'm taking Cubano to our headquarters. Barney and two of Bishop's investigators will drive with me in their cars, we'll leave your car here. You have your evidence kit and camera in it right?"

"Got it Lieu."

Lieutenant Johnson walked over, "Lakeside got their man."

Capanno shook Johnston's hand. "Thanks for all your help, Frank. If you're in our neck of the woods, stop by our station. We'll share our donuts and coffee."

Johnston shook my hand. "Nice job, Kid."

I smiled. "Thank you, Lieutenant."

Capanno continued, his hand still firmly on my shoulder. "I'm going to leave you here with investigators O'Marra and Sanflone. Bishop is getting a search warrant. We need to list exactly what we're looking for in the warrant application: all the items that you are aware of that may be in Cubano's apartment based on your previous visits and knowledge of the facts. Include anything relayed to us by the Varandas."

"We're definitely looking for guns," I said, thinking aloud. "We need several of the trash bags and the twine. Do we have to list the piece of rope holding the curtain back separately? It's in plain view."

"We're going to play it safe and list it." The lieutenant was nodding, acknowledging the items I was recounting.

"I think the twine is especially important. When it's shown in comparison to the piece used to tie one of the girl's hands, it strengthens the probability that the girls were murdered here. We have the piece from the medical examiner's autopsy he removed."

Lieutenant Capanno left to call Bishop, who was waiting to make sure everything that needed to be on the warrant was included.

"We're good," Capanno said when he returned. "I'm heading back now; the others are waiting. Good luck in the apartment, Kid."

The rest of the officers and police vehicles were leaving and the street outside Cubano's building resumed a look of weekday normalcy.

O'Marra approached. "Let's go inside. Bishop radioed Sanflone; he has the warrant."

"What a dump this place is," Sanflone said within a minute of entering Cubano's building.

O'Marra nodded. "State prison will be a step up for that piece of shit."

"I hope he spends a long time there," I said wearily.

"You look tired, Kid," O'Marra said. "How many hours you pushing?"

I had completely lost track of time.

CHAPTER 43

Before we started to search the apartment, Sanflone reminded us, "Bishop said to make sure we stick to what is on the warrant application affidavit. He expects us to keep this case as clean as possible."

"I never went beyond the living area of the apartment, Jack, so I can't tell you what the rest of the place looks like," I said to O'Marra.

We started our search with the washing machines and dryers in the open laundry area of the basement that led to Cubano's apartment.

"I don't think that anybody used these much," I said.

Sanflone nodded. "If you were a tenant, would you come down here? I sure wouldn't venture down here to do laundry."

I opened a lid and looked inside one of the washers. It smelled of dampness and disuse, but held nothing of interest to us.

"Let's move this machine a bit. There's something behind it." Sanflone moved to the other side of the appliance and we pulled the washer forward.

"Oh, God. Is that a *dust bunny*?" Sanflone asked.

"Looks more like a full-grown dust *rabbit*," I said.

It was actually a dirty t-shirt that had been there, gathering dust, for a long, long time.

"I guess we'd better move this search along."

Sanflone took some of the evidence bags that I had brought from my car; I also remembered to bring my camera inside. "Let's put everything we collect in one place in the foyer of the apartment unit. That way, we won't forget anything when we leave." We moved from the basement area into Cubano's apartment.

O'Marra pulled out a pad. "I'll record anything we recover and whatever you photograph, Rocco."

"OK, Jack, but be patient. I have to change the film rolls often. There are only eight exposures on a roll."

Sanflone looked at the camera in my hands. "How many pictures do you plan on taking?"

"Pictures of the items we collect and where we collect them from. I'll get an overall of this room as well. According to the Varandas, this room was the crime scene. The first item I want to collect is the twine holding the curtain back. I'll photograph it where it is and then after we remove it, I'll get a close-up."

"Is that important Rocco?" O'Marra asked.

"I think it's very important, Jack. It looks exactly like a piece taken off one of our victims."

"Jack, write down the photo number, starting at ninety-three, and item description to help match the photos with the evidence lists later."

I took four photos of the room. I photographed the twine and then removed it for the close-up shot. As I did, I said to O'Marra, "Jack, photo ninety-seven, twine on curtain."

I loaded some more film into the camera.

O'Marra looked around and said, "While we're on the subject of twine as evidence, let's get some pictures and samples of the twine on the shelf over there. It's listed on the warrant."

Sanflone nodded. "Let's do the trash bags at the same time, since they're in the same location."

We proceeded to collect samples of twine from the roll on the shelf. We collected two trash bags, one from each of two open boxes near the roll of twine.

"I guess we can't put off exploring this lovely living room," Sanflone said.

I walked around the couch and spotted something not

quite pushed fully underneath. It was a 9mm fully automatic UZI.

O'Marra came over and smiled when he saw the firearm. "I somehow suspect that this is not a legal weapon."

"The idiot didn't even bother to fully conceal it," I said.

"We'll have to thank Cubano for making it easier on us. Nice of him to leave the butt sticking out from his sofa."

"I'll get a picture of how it looks now, sticking out from under the couch, then a close-up of the gun. Jack, you're keeping track of the photo numbers, right?"

O'Marra shot me a look. "Of course, Kid." Then he winked, good-naturedly.

O'Marra lifted the Uzi up to eye level and looked it over. "Obviously he didn't need this to get his morning coffee and newspaper."

A minute later, I opened the drawer of a small lamp table next to the couch. Inside was a Colt 2-inch, 5-shot .38 caliber revolver, along with five dime bags of a white substance, I believed to be cocaine.

"Guns and drugs. Who'd have thought that all this would be going on right here in the Bronx?" O'Marra oozed sarcasm.

As we were checking and rechecking the evidence we collected, making sure we had photos, I took the film processing unit out of a camera-equipment bag.

"What's that for?" Sanflone asked.

"I can develop these slides right here to make sure we haven't missed anything."

"This I have to see," O'Marra said.

Sanflone and O'Marra stood over me, watching, as if they were about to see a magic act.

After I developed the rolls and pulled the film out, the two investigators looked at me, then at each other. O'Marra said, "We have to get this! Rocco, can someone in your department train us to use this stuff?"

"I'm the only guy who seems to know how to use this," I

answered. "And of course, I'd be happy to help. To be honest, if you look at the directions on top of the developer device, every step is printed right here."

O'Marra lifted the developer to look at the directions. "This looks pretty straightforward. I'd like to get one."

I was about to show O'Marra and Sanflone more about the camera and developer when we heard voices coming from the alley.

CHAPTER 44

We looked out the window that faced the alley.
I whispered to the two DA investigators, "During the time I watched this place, not many people came down that alley."

"You think it's our other suspects, Vato and Tramposo?" Sanflone whispered back.

"Could well be."

"Oh, shit," O'Marra said. "We're like fish in a barrel here. Let's wait until they come all the way into the building, close to Cubano's door — if that's where they're heading; we can surprise them the minute they walk inside."

Sanflone shook his head. "No, I think we should wait in the basement to see if they go into the apartment. That way, we'll have an avenue of escape into the alley if we think we need it."

It was agreed. We closed the door to the apartment and ducked behind the washer and dryer in the basement, waiting to see who was approaching.

Two men entered the basement and walked directly toward Cubano's door. One man knocked. "Cubano."

We nodded to each other and stood up. Each of us placing our hands on our holsters.

"Greetings from Westchester County," O'Marra said.

"Who the fuck are you?" the shorter man spun around, surprised.

"No," O'Marra said loudly. "Who the fuck are *you*?"

Sanflone pulled back his jacket with his left hand revealing his badge on a chain around his neck, leaving his right hand on his gun. He held the badge out so that the two men could answer their own question.

"Fuck," the two men whispered, almost in unison.

O'Marra stepped closer to them. "So, let me ask you again. Who are you?"

"Enrique," the taller, and obviously more nervous of the two answered, almost in whisper.

"Enrique, fucking *what*?"

"Huh?"

"Do you have a last name, asshole? Or, are you like Cher?"

"Diaz, Enrique Diaz."

"And you?" Sanflone asked, pointing to the second, shorter man.

Fidgeting, he answered, "Yo soy Bernardo. Bernardo Lopez, soy *Tramposo*."

That nailed it.

"Bernardo, do you speak English?"

"Yes, I speak English good."

O'Marra nodded and said to us, "I guess that's close enough." He turned back to Bernardo. "Then let's answer some questions in English. OK?"

"Okay."

"What are you two doing here?" Jack O'Marra moved closer to Bernardo. He towered over the nervous subject.

Clearly intimidated, Bernardo answered, "Uh...we came to see our amigo, Cubano."

O'Marra turned to me, "Rocco, are these the two you saw *visiting* while you were watching the building?"

I gave Jack a thumbs up, "Looks like them to me, Jack."

"You come here a lot, *Tramposo*?"

"And you, *Vato*." Enrique blinked at the use of his nickname.

"Well, I have some good news," Jack paused for effect, "and some bad news. The good news is that you *are* going to see him. The bad news is that you're both under arrest. Jack then read them their rights.

"Put your hands up where I can see them," Sanflone commanded.

"¿Por que?" Bernardo Lopez asked, sounding – or trying to sound – genuinely baffled.

I drew my gun as Sanflone cuffed Bernardo. I tossed him my cuffs and he quickly slapped them on Enrique's wrists, frisked them both, carefully.

While searching Enrique Diaz, Sanflone found a loaded Smith & Wesson .45 caliber pistol shoved into his waistband. "We have a gun," he said loudly. He handed the gun to me. "Bag it."

"*Por favor*, what did we *do*?" Enrique whimpered.

"You're being charged with suspicion of murder and now we can add weapons possession."

The two men realized that they were in trouble. *Serious* trouble.

You will be going to the Lakeside Police Department. Jack looked at me, then back to Bernardo and smiled, "...upstate."

"You cops are from *upstate*?"

O'Marra had given a nod to the countless times Westchester had been referred to as *upstate*. He shot me a smile. "Yeah. We're like almost from Canada."

"Fucking *Canada*?" Bernardo said, clearly clueless.

"These boys from the Bronx are having a terrible day," O'Marra said before he ordered, "Get against the wall."

I stared at each of the men. "Thanks for stopping by. You saved us the trouble of hunting you down."

When we had the men safely in custody, I radioed headquarters. "Lieutenant, we have our other two suspects in custody."

Capanno couldn't disguise his surprise. "How did you manage that?"

"Believe it or not, Lieu, they came to us. We'll explain when we get there."

"I can't wait to hear this. I'm deploying a marked Lakeside unit with two uniformed officers to your location to pick them up."

"Got it, Lieu."

O'Marra found some old, wooden crates and dropped them on the basement floor. "Sit your asses on these and wait for your ride to Canada."

"We should have run the minute we saw you," Vato said.

"We've been up for over twenty-four hours and we would have been too tired to chase you, Señor Enrique, so if you had tried to run, we would have fucking shot you. Dead!" O'Marra was absolutely serious.

The two men looked down.

"I have a pretty good idea of the car these guys drove here," I said to O'Marra. "I'm going outside to see if there's any vehicle that may belong to them."

Parked in front of the building was an old beat-up former police car, a blue Chevy with a Connecticut plate above the back bumper. I was sure it was the car I saw on DeKalb during my surveillance.

I radioed headquarters and asked them to run the plate. A quick computer check revealed that it was reported stolen out of New Haven, Connecticut. The owner was a cab driver who bought the car at a police auction. Ironically, Vato and Tramposo arrived in a police car and would be leaving in a police car.

I went back and motioned for O'Marra to come outside. "Jack, you're gonna love this. This car came back as stolen. Confirm that the classy Chevy belongs to these assholes."

O'Marra came back outside within a minute or two. "It's their car. Boy, oh boy, possession of stolen property, the list just keeps getting longer."

When I spoke with Capanno he said he would arrange for an authorized tow service to pick up the vehicle."

I was so tired, I literally stumbled back into the basement and fell onto one of the wooden crates to wait for Vato and Tramposo to be picked up and their car to be towed.

Finally, with everything wrapped up, we headed back to

headquarters. Sanflone rode in the tow truck, O'Marra rode with me. "The Lieutenant is anxious to hear every detail," I said. "He's been on this with me from minute one."

O'Marra smiled broadly. "He can wait, Kid. Let's get some coffee."

I returned his smile, "And some doughnuts."

CHAPTER 45

The coffee helped.

I fell into the chair behind my desk, anxious to write the report on the arrests, not more than a couple of lines on the who/what/when/where – and then get some rest.

Lieutenant Capanno came over to my desk as soon as he saw me sit down. "Kid, you did a terrific job, especially considering this was your first homicide case. I still can't believe you pulled it the minute you hit the detective unit."

"Thanks, Lieu."

"Cubano's already been processed, printed and photographed. He's in lock-up awaiting a commitment order to get him to the County jail. After hearing his rights again, he refused to say anything."

"Where are the Varandas?"

"We put them up in the Sandlot Motel in Mayville. e're planning on keeping them there, at least until the grand jury hearing. Andy and Barney are taking care of processing the other two, Lopez and Diaz. They were advised of their rights again as well. Both Diaz and Lopez said they weren't going to say shit."

"Not surprising,"

"Cubano used the prisoner phone; I assume to call a lawyer. Just write your notes on the raid, Rocco. Do the reports tomorrow. There are plenty of people here who can write the processing reports to get all these lovely people to the jail. Computer File 13 arrest data reports will be sent by Sergeant Winston to New York Statewide Police Information Network and the National Crime Information Center."

I noticed that headquarters was crowded and that everyone seemed busy.

"Did you call in the next shift early, Lieu?"

"You've been going nonstop for over a day. Do what you need to and get some rest. Everyone showed, with no bitching. Not Smitty, he's still home in bed with his bad back."

I shook my head and got to my paperwork. In less than an hour I was home and sound asleep. I slept where I had fallen: on top of the bed, still in my street clothes.

Early Thursday morning, I woke up, refreshed from a sound sleep. A long, hot shower, clean clothes, breakfast with Audrey, and I was headed back to headquarters.

The minute I walked in to the bureau, Detective Roberts got up from his desk and approached me. He stood a little closer than necessary, holding his pipe, but not smoking it. "When are you finishing the arrest reports, Kid?"

"Today. The lieutenant just wanted me to get my notes down yesterday before I went home."

As though he was giving me an order, he said, "You *are* going to put Detective Smith on the arrest report, right?"

Maybe it was the built-up stress of the past 36 hours.

Maybe it was the fact that I had come to the conclusion that Roberts had no respect for me. And he certainly had no idea of the number of times *Detective* Smith had been a no-show on the case.

Whatever it was, I snapped.

"Are you out of your fucking mind?" My voice was uncharacteristically loud.

Roberts took a step back, but didn't flinch. "You do remember that it's his case too, don't you?"

"I am very fucking aware that Detective Smith was assigned to be with me during this case. Had he been standing in front of that Bronx doorway with me, facing armed murderers, I'd have no problem putting him in the damned report. But he was NOT there. It will be the proverbial cold day in hell before I include him on this case. He. Was. Not. There. Does that answer your question?"

Roberts turned on his heel and walked back to his desk.

I took a deep breath.

Brian Mason, one of the patrol officers assigned to watch the two Varandas while they were at the motel, approached the desk and asked Sergeant Winston if I was in.

Winston tipped his head in my direction.

"Rocco, you got a minute? I want to fill you in on how the motel detail went." Mason glanced at Detective Roberts, who looked up and glared.

"Okay, Brian. Let's go down to the classroom where we can talk."

I was not going to let my anger at Roberts affect my conversation with Officer Mason. "How're our two babies doing at the motel, Brian?"

"They don't do much talking to me. Most of what they say is to each other — in Spanish — and I don't comprehend." Brian began to laugh, "They'll be in for a shock when one of our officers who does speak the language is on the detail. They speak English when they want to bitch and whine."

"What are they whining about?"

"They are questioning why they are in such a shabby motel. They don't like the sandwiches."

"Compared to what those assholes are used to in the Bronx, the Sandlot should feel like a Hilton. And they're lucky we're feeding them." Then I paused and added with a wink, "You did feed them, right."

Brian put both thumbs up. "Yeah, they get the same wedges we get from Gino's. I don't know what they're used to eating in the Bronx. Did you find any gourmet delicatessens while you were down there?"

"Yeah! Right," I chuckled. "Actually, I was reluctant to even get a coffee. When you get back to the motel, tell them that if they keep bitching, we can throw them in jail with

Cubano. Ask them if they would like jail food better than deli."

Brian laughed. "I don't think they would live long enough to get a meal in a cell with Cubano."

I looked down and shook my head. "It burns me that we have to give these assholes immunity. Unfortunately, their testimony is vitally important for the bigger convictions. Of course, after this case is over, they'll probably go back to their beloved Bronx social club and their reputation as snitches will precede them. Maybe they'll miss the round-the-clock protection they're getting at the Sandlot."

CHAPTER 46

Thursday, June 21st

Andy was on the day shift with me. He wanted to help with the pile of paperwork that had to be done for this case. He sat across from me, working on the reports.-Something was bothering me. "Andy, how come you didn't want to do the arrest detail with me?"

"I'm sorry. I knew that making the arrest was going to take a long stretch of hours." He looked up from his desk. "I wasn't awake enough to be sharp, which could have gotten one of us hurt. Or both of us." He said, steadily. "To be honest, our trip to pick up old man Varanda left me shaking – and I never got out of the van, for God's sake. I haven't felt that unnerved in years. We could have gotten killed. I realized that this case was getting too real, too fast for me. I'm no kid anymore."

"What're you saying? You're not an old man! We were fine, Andy. You know that kind of shit can happen right here in Lakeside, not just the Bronx."

"Yeah, I know it can. But I've made it all these years without anything horrible happening to me and I'm not anxious to push the envelope now."

Scollari continued, "The Bronx part of this is over. I want to help make sure all the I's are dotted and T's crossed so that we get convictions."

"By the way, have you heard from Lieutenant Doore, the great naysayer? He said we would never find out who the girls were; then he said we'd never make any arrests. You sure stuck it up his ass, Kid."

"You're not kidding. And I heard that he's now saying that we'll never get convictions."

"I want to see that jerk's face when those dirt bags are sentenced."

"Okay, let's see what we have to do to put the icing on the cake. I'm glad we worked together on this, Andy. Whether you know it or not, I learned a lot from you."

All the arrest reports were checked and double-checked. The arraignment was scheduled to take place Monday, June 25th in our local courthouse. We were notified that the subjects did have legal representation. It was a given that Ernesto Malino, Enrique Diaz and Bernardo Lopez would be remanded to the county jail without bail. We had no doubt that Cubano and the other defendants would enter *not guilty* pleas and that their lawyers would try to get bail.

Lieutenant Capanno came in to the office a little later that day.

"Paperwork's done, Lieu," I answered his question before he asked. "Should I report back to patrol duty?"

"Let's hold off on that for a couple more days, Rocco. The chief said I should keep you here for a few more days in case the ADA handling the case needs anything."

"Won't Bishop be handling the case, Lieu?"

"No, Bishop's job was to make sure all the procedures for making the case and for making the arrests were followed correctly. The case will be handled by a homicide prosecutor who has more trial experience."

Capanno took a long swallow of the coffee he was holding before he continued. "Even though we have our witnesses set to testify, we have to make sure all the evidence we have supports their testimony."

He took another hit of coffee. "Juries tend to be leery of testimony given by a witness who is getting immunity. The jurors are often suspicious about the motivation and honesty of a witness who was part of the crime. That's why we have to make sure all of our circumstantial evidence lines up to support the testimonies of the Varandas."

I followed the lieutenant into his office. "Do you think we can get a conviction on the evidence we have?"

"It's possible to get a conviction on a strong circumstantial case. But all a defense attorney has to do is raise a reasonable doubt to get an acquittal. You never know how a juror is going to look at circumstantial evidence. But when that evidence is supported by eye-witness testimony, as ours is, it makes for a much stronger case."

"I took a lot of photos for this case, Lieu, and all are developed as slides. Will they be used in court?"

"I'm not sure, Rocco." He looked over the sheets of slides that were on my desk. "We'll find out when we meet the ADA. If not, can we convert them to 8x10's?"

"It's not hard, but it can get costly. The paper used for transferring the slides is a thicker sheet than normal photographic paper; it feels like a thin sheet of rubber. I can produce them here. Do you think I should make prints of all the slides?"

"How many slides do we have?"

"Hundred and ten. Like I said, I took a lot of pictures."

"Oh, shit, no, don't do them all. Do about five, so we can show the ADA what the prints would look like. Be prepared to give a slide show at our meeting and have the ADA tell us which ones he wants."

"Ok, I'll make some that I'm sure will be useful in court. The site where the bodies were dumped, the victims at the morgue before autopsies, and a couple of the crime scene, along with the evidence recovered there should do it."

Capanno nodded. "Sounds good. I'll call the DA's office after the arraignment to see when they would like to meet."

Lieutenant's Capanno's secretary poked her head into the office. "Randy, the Chief wants to see Rocco."

"Oh shit, did I fuck something up?"

"Relax, he probably wants to tell you what a good job you did. Get going."

I walked down the hall and knocked on Chief Silver's door.

"C'mon in," I recognized the chief's gravelly voice.

"Great job, Rocco," Chief Silver said as I entered.

We shook hands.

"Thank you, Chief. I'll feel like the job is finished when these guys are convicted."

"Frankly, there's another reason that I called you in. Winston finally put his papers in. His retirement is effective the end of August. He'll be using some of his accrued vacation time until then. Your promotion will take effect as soon as we can get it approved by the Lakeside Town Board. Winston has to be off the payroll before the promotion request can be submitted. The Chief went on, "I am happy to promote you and happy that I put you in the bureau right before this case popped. You showed us your ability — and your stamina!"

"Thank you, Chief," I said, honored by his words.

"I'm sure the case will go well. Randy tells me it's a strong case." Then he lowered his voice. "I heard that bullshit about how you'd never solve this case."

"You did?"

"Yeah, I know more than people think I know." He smiled. "And I know what a talented cop looks like. Keep up the good work."

"Will do Chief. And again, thank you."

I went back to the detective unit and started to make prints of my slides, my mind uncontrollably switching focus from my work to my promotion.

CHAPTER 47

Monday, June 25th

As expected, the arraignment took place in Lakeside. The three alleged murderers from the Bronx waited on a couch in the main lobby of the new municipal building which, though modern, did not have any holding cells. The men were clearly not happy despite the inviting sign that hung directly over their heads, *Welcome to the Town of Lakeside.* Each prisoner was dressed in an orange jumpsuit, hands cuffed and ankles shackled. Two uniformed police officers stood guard over the prisoners as people entering for everyday business such as tax payments, parking tickets, and building permits, walked by and stared.

Judge O'Neill handled the arraignments of Ernesto *'Cubano'* 'Malino, Enrique *'Tramposo'* Diaz, and Bernardo *'Vato'* 'Lopez.

"Good morning, gentlemen," the Judge said in his characteristic monotone.

"Fuck you all," Cubano said.

"Thank you so much for the greeting." Unflappable, Judge O'Neill read through the standard procedures for arraignment. "The prosecutor, Mr. Carl Renaldo, recommend that you do not receive bail and that you be remanded forthwith to the Westchester County Jail for further proceedings." He looked up and stared at the three men.

"Fuck this upstate, bull-shit town," Cubano said.

Judge O'Neill continued without emotion, "Do you wish to enter a plea to the charges that have been brought against you?"

"Not guilty," Diaz said.

"You?" O'Neill asked Lopez. "No guilty."

"You?" O'Neill asked Cubano.

"Not fucking guilty!" Cubano spit his plea at the judge.

"Thank you. I hereby remand all of you, without the option of bail, to the care and custody of the Commissioner of the Westchester County Department of Corrections." The judge's gavel came down with unquestionable finality.

The men were transported to the county jail.

Within a few minutes, the officers involved in the case were summoned to the DA's office to determine who would provide the key information needed for the grand jury hearing.

Carl Renaldo was the ADA assigned to the trial portion of the case. Mr. Renaldo was relatively young; some defendants and attorneys mistakenly took his boyish looks to indicate a lack of experience. That was a mistake. ADA Renaldo was a seasoned homicide trial prosecutor.

ADA Renaldo addressed us in a conference room one flight up from the courtroom. "The Varandas have been interviewed and prepped for their appearance. My job, now, is to prepare you."

We showed the most relevant slides and the prints I made to the ADA, explaining dates, times and subject matter for each.

"Officer Scollari," ADA Renaldo asked, "Tell me which pictures were taken in your presence."

Andy answered specifically and accurately.

The conversation with Detective Smith did not go as well.

Renaldo showed Smitty a photo of one of the girls on the table at the morgue.

"Detective Smith, who was present when this photo was taken?"

"Me and the kid were there."

"You were in the autopsy room with Officer DeMarco?"

"Well, I wasn't exactly *in* the autopsy room. I was just out-side...waiting to see the evidence."

Detective Smith, can you testify to any of the evidence *as it was gathered* prior to the two autopsy procedures?"

Smitty continued to confuse the issues and frustrate the ADA. "Like I said, I wasn't in the room during the autopsies, Rocco was. I was examining the clothes and stuff from the girls, looking for clues."

Obviously exasperated, Renaldo said, "Did you find any clues?"

"We found some keys in one girl's pocket."

"When you say *we*, do you mean you and Officer DeMarco?"

"Yeah, Rocco was taking pictures of the clothes laid out as they would be when the girls were wearing them. That's when we found the keys."

"OK, I think we have all the information we need. Detective Smith, you are free to leave."

The ADA looked at me. "Officer DeMarco, let me select the slides that I want converted to prints immediately, which I might want as the trial is underway. Remember, the defense is going to want copies of any pictures we introduce into evidence."

"I can make the prints, like the five I gave you, directly from the slides. It will be more involved for the defense to have copies made from prints."

"Good. We'll provide the pictures; they can make copies. Remember, Rocco, give them the pictures, not the slides."

I stood, ready to leave.

"Before you go, Rocco, tell me anything Smith may have done to jeopardize this case. Of course, there is no way I'm putting him on the stand during this trial." He looked directly at me and at Lieutenant. Capanno.

"Your department suffered embarrassment after the

testimony of the Lakeside detectives during our last high-profile case. We were more than lucky we got a conviction."

He did not wait for us to comment. "I'm going to get a video-tape. I want you to see what you're up against." Renaldo left the room and re-entered a moment later. He quickly popped the tape into a waiting VCR. "Our lead defense attorney is addressing new ADAs in New York City on the practice of using police officers as witnesses."

The defense attorney was standing in front of a gathering of new ADAs who were seated in a jury box. "When using police as witnesses," he stated with no lack of certainty, "you have to remember that all cops lie."

ADA Renaldo knew that would get our attention.

"If a police officer is questioned during testimony and he or she does not know or does not remember specifics of a question asked, they are afraid to say, 'I don't know or I don't remember.' They will make something up that sounds plausible." The attorney continued, "In later testimony, after having refreshed their memory with reports or notes, they then amend their original testimony. A defense lawyer need only mention the answer given earlier and say, 'Officer, that's not what you said in your earlier testimony. Did you lie then or are you lying now?' Anything that officer says next remains questionable."

"Shit," Capanno said.

The attorney on the tape strode back and forth in front of the jury box with an air of invincibility. "Remember, all the defense has to do is raise a reasonable doubt. They don't have to prove anything. That burden is on the DA's office. On you."

Renaldo looked at us and said, "Of course not every officer lies or confuses facts on the stand. But we have to remember that the credibility of an officer can certainly raise a reasonable doubt."

Lieutenant Capanno rubbed his forehead. "Is this one of the lawyers defending our defendants?"

"So far, he is only representing Cubano."

"Really," Capanno said. "You've seen Cubano and pictures of the pig sty he lives in. This lawyer in the video comes across as high-priced. Is this a pro bono case or does Cubano have money we aren't aware of?"

"Rest assured, Lieutenant, we'll find out more about their lawyers soon enough. Renaldo turned his attention to me, "Rocco, I'm not going to need you at the grand jury proceedings; we have strong enough evidence to go forward without testimony from you or from Detective Scollari."

ADA Renaldo was not finished. "But Rocco, you will testify at the trial. You were the lead on the case. You were the one present at each stage from the discovery of the bodies to the arrests of all five complicit in the murders: the two Varandas, Cubano, Diaz, and Lopez. And you are present for the current court actions. Make sure you know your facts with absolute accuracy and clarity. I'll see you in court."

Capanno and I left together, neither of us with more to say.

The outcome of the case and the reputation of the department rested squarely on my shoulders.

CHAPTER 48

Monday, October 8th

While I waited for the court date to be announced, the jury to be picked and the trial to begin, I became Sergeant DeMarco and was a squad supervisor in the patrol division.

Despite attention to the demands of my new position, a part of my mind was always on the upcoming trial. My first round of testimony would be related to the discovery of the bodies and evidentiary issues. I knew that some of the investigatory deductions, such as how long the bodies had been left at the crime scene, would be challenged.

I had to be prepared to explain my photographs in detail to the judge to counter objections to them by the defense.

Preparing for testimony, meant reviewing. More than once, Lieutenant Capanno helped me look at the slides and go over my notes. "You're going to be fine in court...Sarge." He was as proud of my new title as I was.

"Thanks, Lieu. You know, there's not much about this case I'll ever forget."

"I get that. I've had cases that I'll never forget. The ones that stay with us usually connect to something that reminds us of something in our own life." He paused and put his coffee mug down on a file cabinet. "What was it about this case for you?"

I thought about his question for a moment. "I've got two daughters."

He nodded. "Then let's do everything we can to prepare. We don't know what the defense might object to. In the past, issues like gory pictures or inflammatory photos have been subject to frequent defense objections."

We went back to reviewing the slides together.

"Rocco, the defense may feel that some photos may anger or excite the jurors. The pictures are graphic." He took a swallow of his coffee, now cold. "Be prepared to explain them or answer questions clearly and objectively. Ultimately, the judge will make the final decision on whether or not to allow them into evidence. I heard that the trial judge will be Judge Michael Carr. By all accounts, he is a fair, no-nonsense man."

Capanno had more news, "The defendants selected to be tried together."

"Really? They had a choice?"

"Yes, they could have made a request to separate the cases. If they had planned on giving testimony against each other, I'm sure they would have wanted separate trials."

"So, if they all requested separate trials, I would have to go through this three times?"

Capanno smiled. "Yup."

CHAPTER 49

Friday, October 26th

I was working the front desk when I received word that the jury had been selected and that the trial date was finally set. In three weeks, the prosecution would make their opening statement. I felt confident that ADA Renaldo would do a good job.

The burden of proof is on the prosecution. In New York, the prosecution presents their opening argument first and presents their closing statement last, after that of the defense team.

Often, the last closing statement is the one the jury takes with them into their deliberations.

I was ready.

And then, just before the start of the trial, we learned that ADA Renaldo would not be prosecuting the case; he had been called away on a family emergency. Another delay.

Lieutenant Capanno broke the news to me. "ADA Anthony Goodman will be taking over. I know Anthony well, we are in good hands."

"Has ADA Goodman been following the case?"

"Yes. In fact, Goodman was present when the grand jury

handed down the indictments. He was going to serve as second chair for the prosecution. The prosecutors in the homicide division are well-qualified, trial-tested lawyers, Rocco. Don't worry."

"Do I need to prepare any differently?"

"No. Anthony will meet with you before you go on the stand for the first time. He will make sure you are prepared for his line of questioning."

I made sure to go over my reports and notes again.

A month later, December 3rd, the trial finally started. It had been almost a year since the bodies of Lola Vasquez and Crystal Ramos had been discovered.

The opening statements were made. Although each defendant had his own attorney, Cubano's attorney, Peter Matson, seemed to be running the show for the defense.

Lieutenant Capanno was the first officer to testify. I was not permitted in the courtroom during his testimony. Afterward, we met in the hallway. "Lieu, is this defense attorney as good as we've been led to believe he is?"

"I wouldn't say he was good as much as cocky. He seems intent on trying to get witnesses to lose their cool and look foolish. In my opinion, I've seen better. I think you'll be fine."

My first appearance on the stand was to be, Wednesday, December 5th. I was scheduled to meet with ADA Goodman in his office at 8AM the day of my appearance. Mr. Goodman was a little older than ADA Renaldo and, even though he initially was going to be second chair, he had a bit more experience in homicide trials than Renaldo had.

ADA Goodman welcomed me into his office from behind his desk. "Have a seat, Sergeant. Everything your department did, all the evidence we submitted, has given us a strong case."

"This is ADA Andrea Davis; she will be second chair."

Goodman leaned forward on his elbows with his chin resting on top of his clasped hands. "Sometimes, I cringe at the thought of putting certain witnesses on the stand. I never know how some people will answer questions, no matter how many times we've gone over their statements together."

"Mr. Goodman, I've testified at trials before. Mostly vehicle and traffic cases or as the first responding officer at the scene of minor crimes. Nothing of this magnitude. This is my first homicide case."

Goodman sat back and looked at me, "Keep your answers short and to the point. The more you say, the more the defense has to question. After I question you, the defense attorney will cross-examine. He will try to discredit your testimony and raise reasonable doubt. If they can discredit the lead investigator on a case, it goes in their favor for an acquittal."

"No pressure then, right?"

"Don't worry. Important point though – during cross examination, don't answer any question too quickly. Look over at our table and pause before answering. It gives time to object to the question and gives you time to think through your response. Once you answer, the bullet is out of the gun, so to speak."

Goodman continued, "Look at the jury when you answer. No matter how much the defense might try to rattle you, maintain your composure. Even though you may want to, no smiling or eye rolling."

"Ok, I'm ready," I said with far more confidence than I felt.

"You'll do fine, Sergeant."

I made sure my uniform was impeccably cleaned and pressed for my appearance in court Wednesday morning. After being sworn in, providing my name, rank and time on the force, ADA Goodman asked a series of questions relating to the discovery of the bodies and eventual focus of our investigation in the Bronx.

"Sergeant, how were the bodies of the girls discovered?"

"County highway workers who were picking up debris on the side of the road discovered that one of the plastic bags that they believed held trash, actually had a body in it."

"How did you become the lead investigator after the discoveries?"

"Lieutenant Capanno and I were the only people working in the detective division that day. He told me to grab a camera and we responded to the scene. After the crime scene was processed, the lieutenant told me that the case was mine."

"And what brought your focus to the Bronx?"

"When I examined the clothing that one of the victims was wearing, I discovered two loose keys."

"What about the keys was instrumental in making the connection to the Bronx?"

I continued to answer the questions calmly and directly. "One of the keys had an imprinted number that indicated it was made by a locksmith on Southern Boulevard in the Bronx." I glanced at Cubano. Perhaps he assumed that he had been careful about removing all identifying items from the girls' bodies.

"How did the Bronx focus become the sole focus of the investigation?"

"Lieutenant Capanno made sure our flyers seeking identification of the victims were sent to New York City precincts, including those in the Bronx."

"And at some point, did that process result in a break in the case?"

"Yes, it did."

"Explain how that happened."

"The mother of one of the victims, Mrs. Ramos, went to one of the housing police precincts, PSA 8, and recognized her daughter's picture on one of our flyers."

"What was Mrs. Ramos' reason for going to the precinct?"

"She was following up on a missing person report she made in early February." I paused, waiting for another question.

"I understand, Sergeant, that Mrs. Ramos was able to provide you with information and photographs that her daughter had taken of friends and people in the neighborhood. Those pictures led to the identification of the accused men. Is that correct?"

"Yes."

"Thank you, Sergeant, I have no further questions at this time."

I had done well.

When I had time to look at the defense table, I saw that the defendants had been cleaned up for the trial. Cubano and his co-defendants wore suits and ties. Carefully groomed, Cubano no longer looked like a brutal killer. The defense was trying their best.

The attorney who Lieutenant Capanno and I had watched on Mr. Renaldo's tape, Mr. Peter Matson, was indeed representing Cubano. Lopez and Diaz each had his own attorney seated at the defense table. Matson seemed to be the only one taking notes during my testimony. I was ready for this lawyer.

But first we adjourned for lunch.

CHAPTER 50

We returned from lunch, court was again in session. I was back on the witness stand ready for the cross examination to begin. Mr. Matson took his time getting up from his seat. He slowly approached the witness stand, his hands in his pockets.

He looked at me and smiled, as if ready to have a friendly chat. "I see by your uniform you are a sergeant."

I paused before I answered. "Yes, I am."

"Were you a sergeant at the start of this case?"

I paused again and when I looked, I saw that ADA Goodman was not happy with that question, but he didn't object.

"No, I wasn't."

"What was your rank?"

Again, no objections. "I was a police officer."

"Aren't you all police officers?"

He was trying to rattle me.

"Yes, we are all police officers," I answered steadily.

"So, what was your rank?"

"The rank below sergeant is police officer. With more women on the force, the title of *patrolman* was changed to *police officer.*"

"Were you a detective?"

I took my time before I answered, as Goodman instructed.

ADA Goodman rose. "I object, Your Honor. The officer has already made it clear that the rank he held at the beginning of this case was that of police officer."

Judge Carr nodded. "Objection sustained. Move on, Mr. Matson."

"Sergeant, is it common practice for a police agency to assign such an important case to a police officer?"

Goodman stood again. "I object, Your Honor. Counsel is asking this witness to be familiar with the practices of all police agencies."

"Objection sustained. Rephrase your question, Mr. Matson."

"Sergeant, is it common practice for the Lakeside Police Department to assign a murder case to someone who is not a detective?"

"I object, Your Honor," Goodman bellowed. What is the relevance of Mr. DeMarco's rank?"

Carr leaned back in his chair. "I'll allow it. Sergeant, you may answer the question."

"At the start of the case, I was assigned to the detective division. That's why I got this case."

"But are officers, who are not detectives, assigned to murder cases?"

The ADA was obviously getting annoyed. I followed his instructions and remained calm and paused before answering.

Once again, Goodman rose. "Your Honor, we have already determined the rank of this officer. The facts have been established: he was working out of the detective division and he was assigned this case. Unless defense is insinuating that some departmental policy was violated, I suggest we are finished with this line of questioning."

Judge Carr agreed. "Counselor, move on."

"Sorry, Your Honor." Matson looked back at me and paused. "Sergeant, did you meet with the assistant district attorney prior to your testimony?"

"Yes."

ADA Goodman shook his head. "Your Honor, defense is trying to suggest some procedural impropriety has taken place. It is common for witnesses for the prosecution to meet with us before the trial."

"I'll rephrase. Sergeant, *when* did you meet with ADA Goodman?"

"This morning, before the trial started.

"Is that the first time you met with him?"

After a pause, "Yes."

"You haven't met with ADA Goodman prior to today?"

"No sir."

"Isn't it true," Matson said, raising his voice a bit, "you met with this ADA during your grand jury testimony?"

"I didn't testify at the grand jury hearing, sir." I looked at the jury and then back at Mr. Matson. He had made a mistake.

"Counselor," Judge Carr said. "Do you have any more questions for this witness?"

"No further questions at this time, Your Honor."

"You may step down, Sergeant. Remember, if you are called back to the stand, you are still under oath."

"Yes, Your Honor, I understand."

I had weathered round one. And won.

Two days later, I returned to the stand to answer questions about photographs that were being entered as evidence. Just as the lieutenant had predicted, the defense had objections to some of the images.

Judge Carr had the jurors removed from the courtroom until after he ruled on the photographs.

Matson objected to a close-up shot of Lola Vasquez's hands and how they were tied. The photo showed that the twine used to tie her hands would match the piece we took from Cubano's apartment. It was the twine that held back the drapes.

Judge Carr asked Mr. Matson to explain his objection.

"Your Honor, I believe this photo is inflammatory. It shows the girl's hands tied so tightly that her nails turned blue."

Judge Carr leaned back. "Sergeant, please explain the photo."

"Your Honor, the subject of the photo is the twine, which is a key piece of evidence. The victim's nails are blue because that is the color of her nail polish."

The judge nodded. "The photo is admitted. Do you have objections to any of the other photos, Counselor?"

Matson's objections were overruled and the jury was returned to the courtroom.

The photo of the twine, when compared to the piece taken from Cubano's apartment, served to put the victims in Cubano's apartment at the time of the murders.

Before I walked out of court at the end of the day, I watched as the Court Officers put Cubano back into handcuffs.

CHAPTER 51

During the next few days of the trial, Andy and DA investigators, Jack O'Marra and James Sanflone were called to testify. I was not permitted in the courtroom since I could be recalled to the stand.

I met with Mr. Goodman in his office late one afternoon after court had been adjourned.

"How did the Varandas do?" I asked him.

"Danny was the first to testify. He didn't do too badly during my direct examination. He was nervous as hell, though. And, because he's not too bright, questions had to continually be rephrased or explained."

"Was his testimony consistent with the statement he gave us after his arrest?"

"Yes. He was well-prepared and he stuck to his story despite his obvious fear. He couldn't even glance at the defense table. Cubano's hot-shot lawyer was the first defense lawyer to go after him. He was relentless. The young Varanda was rattled. In fact, I can't remember objecting to a counselor's questions to one witness that many times ever before."

"What kind of questions did he ask?"

"That's why there were so many objections. He was making accusations instead of asking questions. The lawyers representing the other two defendants, Diaz and Lopez, were from Legal Aid and took their turns getting into Danny's face. They were not as dramatic as Cubano's lawyer, but they also made him sweat."

"What about the father, Pablo Varanda?"

"He was a bit more composed, did a good job. He still had fear in his eyes and, at one point, he did look over at the defense table. I believe Cubano's lawyer intentionally asked him some questions from the defendants' table to make him look in that direction. Matson tried to insinuate that the Varandas did the killings."

"Did you detect any reactions from Cubano and the others?"

"If looks could indeed kill, Mr. Pablo Varanda would have been a corpse on the witness stand."

Goodman reflected for a minute before he continued. "Each of the Varandas gave compelling testimony. I am convinced that their cooperation had less to do with getting themselves out of trouble and more to do with the fact that they didn't want to see Cubano and his group ever get out of prison. The jury seemed attentive and I'm sure they were aware of the defense tactics to incriminate Danny and his father. I wonder if any juror figured out what a no-win situation those two were in."

"I agree with you regarding the Varandas' motivation to keep Cubano and his buddies locked up. I can't help but think that Cubano's two co-defendants are not the only low-life characters he associates with."

"I was thinking about that, too," Goodman said.

"The Varandas may not have a long-life expectancy with or without Cubano on the street."

Goodman looked out the window. "You know what, Rocco? I don't give a shit. I want convictions. Do you care what happens to them?"

"Hell, as far as I'm concerned, they're just as guilty as the other three."

"I think our case is strong. Our witnesses' testimonies corroborated our evidence. Let's see how long the jury takes to deliberate after they are given their instructions from Judge Carr."

CHAPTER 52

Tuesday, December 13th

The trial lasted two weeks.

The jury reached their verdict after one day of deliberation. Each of the defendants was found guilty on two counts of murder in the second degree.

Cubano, Lopez, and Diaz were remanded into custody until the sentencing, Monday, December 17th.

I was excused from work to witness the sentencing.

I arrived at the courthouse with Lieutenant Capanno and Andy. When we entered I saw Detective Angel Canazzaro. He had taken Mr. and Mrs. Ramos up for the sentencing. Mrs. Vasquez declined his offer. Lieutenant Capanno, Andy and I sat in the front row of the spectators' area, directly behind the defense table. I wanted the three defendants to see us in the courtroom.

Judge Carr took some time before he spoke. "I've been a judge for many years and the depravities of some of the cases I see don't surprise me anymore. But *this* particular case is one I would put toward the top of the list of heinous offenses. The defendants will rise."

"You have each been found guilty of two counts of murder

in the second degree. If I could give each of you the death penalty, I would. Since that is not an option, I am sentencing each of you to two consecutive sentences of twenty-five years to life. Your terms will be in a state correctional facility yet to be determined. You will be remanded to the county jail until you are transferred to prison. I would like to take this opportunity to thank the jurors for their service." And, as an exclamation point Judge Carr slammed his gavel and said, "Court is adjourned."

I knew for Cubano, at least, his would be a life sentence since he was already fifty-one years old.

When the judge rose, Cubano turned his head and looked directly at me. He made a throat-cutting movement with his thumb, a death threat.

I smiled and thought to myself that I would be sure to keep my eye open for a 101 year old man coming after me, in fifty years.

EPILOGUE

The conclusion of our successful investigation and the convictions of the people responsible for this crime were bitter-sweet. Justice prevailed, however, the sentencing of Cubano and his accomplices would not bring Lola or Crystal back to their families.

As I was putting my material together after the sentencing, I came across the photos Mrs. Ramos had given me. A quick phone call assured me that Mrs. Ramos was at home. I gathered the photos and drove down to her apartment to return them.

When Maria Ramos opened the door, she greeted me with a hug.

"Thank you so much for making sure the men who took our Crystal from us got punishment. I am sorry, my husband had to be at work. I am sure he would want to be here to thank you. ¿Usted puede quedarse para el café?"

"Don't apologize, I know your husband works hard. And thank you, I would be pleased to stay for a cup of your coffee."

I took the pictures out of the envelope I had put them in and handed them to Mrs. Ramos. She teared-up for a moment when she saw the pictures of Crystal. Then she smiled, "The coffee will keep you awake, no?"

"Don't worry, I will sleep just fine knowing Cubano and his amigos will be in jail for a very long time."

As I was leaving Mrs. Ramos said, "Muchas gracías. Ve con Dios."

I took her hand and said, "And may God be with you and

your family as well."

When Lieutenant Capanno retired, a few years after the homicide case closed, I advanced to the rank of lieutenant and was assigned charge of the detective division. Lieutenant Capanno left me with a crop of new, young detectives. My responsibility was to provide guidance, supervision and support for them.

One of my older detectives was Detective Thomas O'Malley. During the years after our first joint investigation of the Stevens' burglary, Tom proved to be an excellent police officer with great powers of observation, the ability to come to reasoned deductions, and good people skills. I was happy to have him in my division.

. One day as I was going into the luncheonette in downtown Lakeside, I happened to run into Andy. He didn't seem to age; he looked as fit as the day he retired.

"Let's get some coffee, Andy. I know a good place, highly recommended by Detective Smith."

Andy started to laugh, "Have you seen him lately?"

"I did," and started to laugh myself. He still calls me *Kid*."

Andy and I talked some more over coffee. It felt, as it always did, like old times. And as we were leaving, he added, as he always did, "You did great, "Kid."

CPSIA information can be obtained
at www.ICGtesting.com
Printed in the USA
BVHW081934090323
660095BV00006B/188